CW00521189

The Sail Loft

Andy Grant Sawyer

The Sail Loft

Copyright © Andy Grant Sawyer 2004

ISBN: 1 903607 57 4

All rights reserved. No part of this publication may be reproduced, transmitted, or stored in a retrieval system, in any form or by any means, electronic, mechanical, photocopying, recording or otherwise, without prior permission in writing of the author.

Published by Able Publishing 2004

Typesetting and production by:

Able Publishing
13 Station Road
Knebworth
Hertfordshire SG3 6AP

Tel: (01438) 813416 / 812320
Fax: (01438) 815232
Email: books@ablepublishing.co.uk
www.ablepublishing.co.uk

To Kate, James and Nick

Remembering happy holidays
in Cornwall

Acknowledgements

To Jan for typing up my original notes and giving me the push to publish.

To Chrissie for the final draft and staying calm amongst the alterations.

Ben Treloar bent his head towards the spray blowing in from the sea and shuffled along the path that led to his cottage. He fumbled in his coat pocket for the back door key but it was not there.

It was then that he remembered that he had left it in the teapot on the dresser in the kitchen. What a fool I am, he thought to himself as he lifted the latch and opened the door. It had been open all the time! Once inside he switched on the light, threw a log on the fire and sat down in the nearest chair.

The day had been a hard one. Clearing out his Aunt's cottage had been more difficult than he'd imagined. It was all well and good her going to live in America with her daughter, but she needed to make a decision about what she was taking and what she was leaving.

It was strange how he'd known his Aunt for so long and lived near her for the past five years and yet had rarely been inside her cottage. Every room was different from the other. There was no pattern to the way she lived or any connection between any of the rooms. His Aunt's way of life had been ordered but in such a way as to prevent Ben from seeing her clearly as a particular character. Now she was going, so he would never know anyway and he put the thought out of his mind and went to bed.

The next day was very different, and in many ways the start of a new life for Ben.

He got up early as usual, you couldn't help it with the gulls crashing about on the roof, and sat in the garden eating his breakfast. The grass was damp, a touch of autumn already, and a slithering mist hung over the harbour below. Thin plumes of smoke rose like needles, where other early risers had lit their fires. Even in summer the solidly built stone cottages could be bitterly cold and damp.

Ben liked it here, and was glad he'd made the long thought over and discussed decision to move to the place of his childhood memories. At last he was free from the stresses and strains of life up country. He was financially worse off, but he had the cottage, the view, the people and a much more satisfying way of life.

He wasn't so sure about his Aunt moving. After all, it was the last link with his immediate family – was she really leaving him to sort everything out for her? Surely some of what was in the house must hold memories for her. She seemed adamant, however, that Ben should sort it, sell it, and gain some profit from her move. "Only the basics" she kept telling him, "nothing more. I need only the basics. After all, it's my daughter's house I'm moving to and she's enough junk of her own."

Ben finished his breakfast, looked at his watch and strolled down to the harbour. The Estate Agent was coming at ten so there was just time to buy a paper, watch the fishing boats put out to sea and climb back to his Aunt's cottage. She didn't even seem interested in who was going to buy the cottage and live there when she'd gone.

The sun was out now and somehow to Ben the whole scene appeared unreal, as if he was watching a film in slow motion, or was it just that this was his dream fulfilled. It was almost ten. What was the Estate Agent's name? He couldn't remember.

As he approached his Aunt's cottage a car drew up beside him.

"Excuse me."

He turned, caught in his own thoughts and replied "Yes."

"Can you direct me to Mrs Treloar's cottage?"

Ben bent slightly and looked down at the face peering from the car window. His mouth must have dropped open as she repeated her question.

"Can you tell me where Mrs Treloar lives?"

"Oh yes, I'm sorry. I'm her nephew. It's me you've come to see er…I'm Ben Treloar. You'll have to park your car next to the harbour and walk. I'll show you the way.

"Thank you."

She smiled and followed his directions to the car park.

He watched as she got out of the car, her hair steaming back off her face as the wind caught it. She turned and smiled again, a smile that caught his breath and made him shiver all over. She locked the car and walked purposefully towards him. It wasn't just the smile that had made him feel like that, it was the eyes. Dark, piercing eyes that shimmered in the sunlight. They were bright, lively and as she neared him, he saw sensuality in them too.

"Hi, I'm Joanna Trewick. You're Mrs. Treloar's nephew did you say."

"Yes, it's good to meet you. I…well…you see…"

"You're handling the sale of her house?" Joanna interrupted him as he hesitated.

How stupid of me, he thought. She must think I'm an idiot.

"Yes I am. The cottage is just round the corner."

They walked in silence until the whitewashed cottage came into view.

"There are still some of her belongings inside. I'm in the middle of sorting it all out for her."

"Your Aunt's not here at the moment?"

"No, she's visiting relatives. So I've got the run of the place."

"Do you live here too?"

"Oh no, I've my own place up the hill. It's much smaller and suits me fine."

They reached the front door and Ben turned the key in the lock and stood back to allow Joanna to walk inside.

It was dark coming in from the sunlight outside and they

both blinked and took a while to adjust. The cottage still had that fresh smell about it that his aunt was so proud of and the sun threw patterns across the flowered wallpaper. Joanna walked around making notes and taking measurements. Ben wandered into the kitchen at the back and put the kettle on.

"Coffee?"

"Yes please, but do you mind if I look round first?"

"No, help yourself. I'll give you a shout when it's ready."

"Thank you. How many rooms upstairs?"

"Three and a bathroom."

"Thanks."

Joanna smiled again and went upstairs.

Ben returned to his thoughts. That smile really was quite wonderful. Did she have a ring on? Married, engaged, he couldn't decide and there was no way he was going to ask. The kettle boiled just as she came down the stairs. Ben poured the water onto the coffee in two outsize mugs. They were kept especially for workmen and everything else was packed away.

"What's out the back?"

"Oh just the small yard, garden and the Sail Loft."

"What exactly is the Sail Loft?" she asked

"A glory hole really. My Aunt's husband used it for years as a workshop before he died. When they moved in here it was full of sails and fishing equipment. I've still got to sort that out."

"Interesting. It'll make quite a difference to the sale price. Pity it's not attached to the main building."

"Well it is in a way," replied Ben, "this door leads directly into it."

He turned and pointed to a small door, barely five foot high that was hidden by the dresser. He moved a chair out of the way and opened the door.

"There you are. It's a bit dark, the light bulb's gone. You're welcome to walk through. I could get my torch."

"I think I'll have the coffee first, please."

"Milk and sugar?" enquired Ben.

"Just milk thanks" she replied as she sat down at the table. "This is nice. Is it oak?"

"Yes, my Aunt brought it here when they moved. It's from an old farm house near where they used to live."

"So what do you do?" Joanna asked, changing the subject.

"Ah, well…not an awful lot really. People in the village think I don't work at all."

"You must do something surely?"

"Yes, I make pots and paint a little, watercolours, but I'm not very good."

"That sounds wonderful. Did you have a lot of training?"

"No. I went to evening classes for the pottery although I'd done the basics at college."

"What sort of college?"

"Teacher. I trained as a teacher in Arts. That's what I did before I moved down here."

The conversation continued like this for some time with Ben recounting his past life and how he'd made the decision to move to the South West. His parents had died and left him a small amount of money, which had made up his mind for him. That was how he had ended up in his cottage, doing, at last, what he wanted.

Ben hadn't talked to anyone about his reasons for moving before, not even his Aunt. She had just accepted that he was there. Joanna was different. She seemed unusually interested or was she just being polite. He knew nothing about her. Dare he ask?

"Have you always worked as an Estate Agent?"

"Yes, straight from school really. I've worked my way up."

"You've never thought of doing anything else then?"

"Of course I have. I went to London for a while. I wanted to go to University, but I messed up my A levels. Too much time surfing! Can we look at the Sail Loft now please?"

"Yes of course. I'm sorry. I've kept you talking far too long. You must have other clients to meet."

"No, I'd set the morning aside for this. I'll follow you."

They walked through the narrow passage, which was lit by small windows, and into the Sail Loft. Ben had forgotten just how cluttered it was, but Joanna's mouth dropped open.

"My goodness, it's wonderful. Wherever did all this come from, it must be worth a fortune?"

Ben looked at what he largely considered to be junk and back at Joanna's face. Her eyes were flickering from object to object in absolute amazement.

"How many rooms like this are there?"

Well there's this one and one beyond, which has a staircase leading to a further two above."

"Are they all full like this?"

"Oh yes, it's very hard to get through. Why, do you want to look upstairs too?"

"Yes, I'd love to. I'm not stopping you doing anything else am I?"

"No, not at all. Follow me."

Ben pushed an old bike out of the way to give Joanna more space and opened the door to the next room. This was lit by a huge window which looked back at the kitchen, but received plenty of sunlight from over the roof. Joanna's eyes still kept flashing around the room, obviously taking in every item and recording them somewhere in her mind. She still held her notebook and occasionally wrote notes in between brushing dust and cobwebs from her suit. Ben had reached the stairs and started to climb.

"Are you OK Joanna?" he asked, realising he ought to have said Miss Trewick. Somehow Joanna seemed the right thing to say. He felt very relaxed in her company.

"Yes, thank you. Are these stairs safe? They look very rickety."

"Yes, they're fine," Ben replied, "just mind your head on the ceiling as you reach the top."

The two upstairs rooms were crammed full too, but there seemed to be some sort of order. Boxes were labelled, furniture carefully covered and arranged in a way that you could find something you wanted easily.

His Uncle must have done this, thought Ben. After all, his Aunt was much more disorganised and was probably responsible for the mess downstairs.

Joanna seemed impressed and was still making notes, but Ben failed to see what relevance all this could have to the sale of the house.

"Have you seen enough?" Ben asked casually.

"Yes, I think so. Those boxes intrigue me though. Do you know what's in them?"

"No, I've never really been up here before. They're going to be quite a problem when I eventually get to sort them out, there's so many."

"Yes, you'll need some help I should think" Joanna replied quickly.

Ben turned away from her and led the way back down the stairs. Was she angling to help or was it genuine curiosity? Maybe she's hoping to see what's in the boxes in order to bump up the price of the cottage. Sell everything with it. He didn't know what to say so they walked back to the kitchen in silence.

Joanna spoke first.

"Thank you for showing me round, oh, and the coffee. I'll have to go back to the office and work everything out. I'll phone a price through and then confirm in writing. Here or your place?"

"Pardon?"

"Where shall I phone, send the confirmation?"

"Oh, sorry. You'd better send it to me. I'll write the address down for you and the phone number."

"Thank you."

Joanna put out her hand and they shook hands. She smiled and Ben noticed her eyes again. They really were terrific.

"It's been very nice meeting you, Mr Treloar, thanks again, Bye."

"Bye," Ben replied meekly as he closed the door behind her. She really was quite something. He'd never met anyone quite like her. Those eyes, the smile, and so easy to talk to. The same thoughts kept going through his mind.

He washed up the mugs, idly noticing the one with lipstick and washing it rather more slowly than his own. Ben sat down at the kitchen table, as he dried the mugs and stared across the courtyard at the Sail Loft. He began to wonder too about the boxes so neatly arranged and what Joanna had said. How could he possibly sort all this out before his Aunt left? She really was a nuisance leaving so soon. What if someone bought the cottage quickly, he may never know what was in the Sail Loft, and Joanna was right, he would need help. Was she offering or was it just business talk? How could he tell?

Ben locked up, having remembered to pick up the paper he'd bought earlier and walked back up the hill to his cottage.

He made himself some lunch and sat out in the garden, where he watched next door's cat chasing butterflies across his lawn.

The newspaper didn't hold his attention for long either. Something was making him unsettled and he couldn't put his finger on it. He got up and went over to his shed, opened the door and checked his kiln. It had switched itself off, but it was still too hot to inspect his handiwork. Ben called it his shed but it was more like an outhouse partly attached to the house, but it served his purpose.

He sat down at his table and fiddled with a piece of clay that was really too dry to work properly. Even this, which he usually enjoyed so much, did not hold his attention for long.

He got up again, cleaned his hands, went back into the garden and shouted at the cat to clear off. It didn't.

The phone rang. Ben ran into the living room and picked it up.

"Hello. Oh it's you. How are you? Yes, the Estate Agent came this morning. No, she's going to ring back with a price. Yes, and confirm in writing. All right, I'll see you later in the week. Yes, I'll let you know. Bye."

Ben put the phone down. He went back into the garden, sat down and finished his lunch whilst reading the paper. He realised his unease was Joanna's fault. He was waiting for a call and had hoped it was her and not his Aunt. She really had made an impression on him. He felt silly, like a schoolboy with a crush on someone in his class, to whom he couldn't explain his feelings. How stupid, he thought. Joanna might not even phone today, she's got other people to see. She's probably like that with everyone. It'll be her training – be pleasant to everyone! No. he wasn't convinced. Surely there was something else there too. He'd felt it, had she too. Ben knew he must see her again, but had he the nerve to make the first move?

These thoughts stayed with him all afternoon. Ben couldn't settle to any work so he wandered back down to the harbour just to see who was around. He knew a few locals really well now and some he was on nodding acquaintance with, but to most he was still an in-comer and to be excluded from all that was considered traditionally of local interest. His closest friend he considered to be George Barton, who had also once been a teacher and returned to his native Cornwall some years ago. He had welcomed Ben as soon as he moved in, perhaps because he saw in Ben a younger version of himself. George now ran a bookshop in the village with his wife, but preferred taking his boat out fishing as much as possible.

Very early in their relationship George had taught Ben to fish and more importantly how to manage a boat. George was determined that Ben would one day purchase his own and enjoy the freedom, and peaceful outings, beyond the harbour wall.

George's boat, however, was not moored in the harbour, so that avenue of possibilities dried up.

There was only one thing for it, he'd have to go home and do some work. If he didn't make anything, there'd be nothing to sell through the local craft shops. This time he managed to finish five bowls and three vases, before deciding that an evening meal ought to be started.

It was whilst eating this later and going over the events of the day, that the first seeds of an idea were sown, regarding the future of the Sail Loft. It was something Joanna had said. She was so ecstatic about the Sail Loft and it's contents. Perhaps there was something of importance there or was it the building she was really enthusiastic about. He went over and over what had happened. What he had always considered to be junk would have to be looked at in a new light, Joanna had seen to that!

He looked around his own home and compared it with his aunt's. If he moved into her cottage he'd have more space to work in, be nearer the harbour and perhaps even use the sail loft for his pottery. No, his Aunt wouldn't agree to it, after all she needed the money from its sale. He certainly couldn't afford to buy it, but then how much would it cost? Joanna hadn't phoned after all, so he still had no idea.

Ben went to bed that night still trying to work out what to do, but of one thing he was sure. Tomorrow he would clear out the sail loft.

That night he slept badly. He was confused. Had to make a decision. Which was the right way to go? After all, he had what he'd always wanted, but had he?

Was this the right cottage to be in or should he move again? No. He had his pottery, his own home and his garden. The sail loft only had a courtyard. Where could he grow his plants?

Why was Joanna so keen on the building? What had she seen that he hadn't?

So many thoughts and images flashed through his mind that night. By the morning he felt exhausted, drained, but marginally clearer in his own mind about which decision to make.

He got up and strolled into the garden. He stood and let his eyes absorb every inch of it. He flicked stems and petals with his fingers. His hands caught droplets of water as they cascaded from leaves, sparkling in the early morning sun. This was where he felt at home, peaceful and calm. Free to think his own thoughts, make his own decisions.

That jolted him back to reality and what he must do.

He walked back inside, picked up Joanna's card and dialled the estate agent's number. No answer. He looked at his watch. Too early. He'd try again later.

Breakfast. He threw half of it away. No appetite. He looked at his watch again. Still too early.

He sat down and let his eyes wander around the room taking in it's every aspect. Did he really want to leave this so soon? He got up again and went back into the kitchen and put the kettle on. Maybe a cup of coffee would clear his mind and the way to go would become more clear.

Almost immediately the phone rang. It was his aunt.

"Yes. No. She hasn't....I've tried but there was no reply. I need to talk to you about the house anyway. I've had an idea. I know it's not your phone, this is important. I'll phone you back. Yes...Now."

He had been thinking as he spoke to his aunt. What to do had suddenly become clear. He knew what he must do.

He made the coffee, checked the phone number and dialled. It was a long call. He explained in detail what his plans were. Fortunately his aunt listened, without her usual interruptions, until he had finished. There was a pause.

"Yes Ben. I agree. What a lovely idea. You go ahead. I'll see you when I get back. Let me know how you get on with the estate agent. Bye."

Ben put the phone down, sipped his coffee and walked into the garden. It was raining. He watched the raindrops bouncing off the surface of his coffee, glanced around his garden, turned, smiled and went inside.

He picked up the phone again and dialled...

"Joanna Trewick please...Oh Hi, its Ben Treloar."

"Ah, I was going to contact you this morning, I've a price for you."

"I think I need to see you again to discuss a slight change of plan." Ben said hesitatntly, not really really sure what to say.

"Oh right. Let me see. I'm free this afternoon at two. Could you come into the office then?"

"Yes that's fine. I'll see you then. Bye."

Ben put down the phone and realised he was sweating profusely. Joanna certainly had an effect on him and that was only over the phone.

Now he had made the first move forward into the future. He was more certain of what he wanted and where he wanted to be, but he had to see if the financial side would work out first.

There was, however, one thing he must do before he saw Joanna again. The Sail Loft. He must take another look and check exactly what was there.

Ben walked down to his Aunt's house taking in the view across the harbour, the sun reflecting off the water and the sounds of the squawking gulls above his head.

He stopped in the middle of the car park and stared wistfully out at the island beyond the harbour wall. The tide was in and waves spilt over the edge of the island and a boat bobbed up and down nearby.

The thought of the Sail Loft drifted from his mind as the

reason he'd moved here overwhelmed him. The job, the friends, the one real close friend who'd encouraged him to do what he really felt was right. He'd listened, he thought and he'd been confused. Finally, he'd made the decision to move, to leave all that had gone before.

Still caught up in his thoughts he walked to the harbour café, sat at a table in the corner and stared out of the window. Once again, the sun's reflection caught his eye. He blinked, squinted and turned to look at the menu.

Why, he didn't know, as he often came in here and knew the menu off by heart.

"Hello Ben, can I get you anything?"

It was Jenny, the owner of the café.

"Yes, thanks. I'll have coffee and a toasted teacake please Jenny."

"Do you want jam with that like you usually do?"

"Yeah…I'll have raspberry, as usual!" Ben replied.

He returned to looking out of the window. Doubt swept over him as he contemplated his planned move to his Aunt's cottage. Was this really what he wanted? What was it about Joanna that made him feel unsettled, but needing to see her again? He loved where he lived, the cottage, the garden, his pottery, but above all else the tranquillity. His Aunt's cottage had none of this, but it did have the Sail Loft. The Sail Loft and its contents which seemed to draw him ever nearer to a move. Whilst lost in these thoughts, Jenny had brought his coffee and teacake, but he hadn't noticed.

Now the sea seemed to have taken on a different guise. It looked muted, without power or purpose and the gulls no longer swooped down low over it's swell. He didn't seem to notice the time passing. His coffee was now lukewarm and the teacake soggy. He didn't enjoy it.

He got up, paid and left the café behind him. As he ambled along the top of the harbour wall he looked longingly up the hill to his own cottage. He would go back there and make a final decision. The boxes in the Sail Loft could wait. After all, he had to see Joanna at two o'clock. Before that he would have to have a clear idea in his head about his future plans.

The walk back up the hill was slow and laborious. Ben kept stopping and looking back towards his aunt's cottage and then out to sea, as if the answer lay somewhere beyond the harbour wall.

He pushed open his front door, slumped in the settee and stared blankly into the fireplace. He did love it here. It was, at last, a home of his own, where he could relax and be himself. No-one hanging on his decisions, no deadlines to meet and certainly not the same pressures. This could be an idyllic life, but was he being selfish? What about all the people he'd left behind? No, he had made the break, it was his choice and now there was another to be made. What to do about the Sail Loft.

He got up again and sauntered through to the kitchen, opened the back door and stepped into the garden. Although it was now later in the morning, the grass was still damp and he stood taking in every sight, smell and sound. This garden was a haven of peace. He loved it. It was perfect.

Somehow, he knew what he must do. He looked at his watch, noted the time, locked up the cottage and walked back down the hill to the bus stop. Buses ran fairly frequently but he never seemed to reach the bus stop at the right time. He looked around for a familiar face. None was forthcoming. He leant over the railings and stared once more out towards the island. Somehow, the island seemed larger than usual, as if it had risen further from the sea whilst he'd been in the café.

He imagined it rising still further like a new volcano, with a turreted castle perched precariously on top. From the castle rode knights with armour glinting in the sunlight and long flowing robes flapping in the breeze.

The bus screeched to a halt behind him. It always did. Maybe it was the salt getting into the brakes.

"Return please" he mumbled as he handed over his money. He sat halfway down the bus and glanced at the island again. No castle, no knights, just breaking waves and gulls. Now he must get his mind onto the matter in hand. His cottage and his Aunt's cottage and of course seeing Joanna again.

The bus journey into town seemed to take forever. There was someone either getting on or off at every stop. Ben got off at the Old Courthouse, as he always did, and crossed the road before walking the few yards to the Estate Agents. He stopped outside and took a deep breath. Apart from his move to the area, this was going to be his biggest decision. A decision that would shape his future life.

He pushed open the door, walked in and looked around. No sign of Joanna. He fixed his gaze on a blonde girl sitting at a desk near the window.

"I have an appointment with Miss Trewick at two o'clock. Is she here?"

"Ah, you must be Mr Treloar. She left a message for you. I have it here. She's very sorry but she's had to go to Truro on urgent business. She'll contact you when she gets back. Oh, and she left this valuation for you." The girl handed over a sealed envelope with his name printed clearly on the front.

"Do you have any idea at all when she'll be back?"

"Not today, certainly. Sometimes she's away for weeks. It rather depends on how important the sale is. I can't help you any more than that. I'm sorry."

"It's alright. At least I have the valuation. Thanks for your help."

Ben left the Estate Agents and sauntered down the road idly opening the envelope as he went. He took the enclosed letter out and flipped it out flat, reading the print carefully. His eyes leapt down the page to the figures in bold type. He knew house prices had risen a lot since he moved there, but he couldn't believe what he was seeing. The price was much better than he'd expected and how could Joanna have valued the contents of the Sail Loft without really looking at what was there?

He'd only paid £60,000 for his cottage. Admittedly it wasn't on the harbour side like his Aunt's but even so it did seem excessive. The extra for the contents bothered him too. Joanna had added on a further £10,000 for them. What had she seen there, or rather, what had he missed?

Ben decided to go back to his Aunt's and have a really good search through everything. Again, the bus took ages to come, but once on it, the return journey was much quicker.

Back inside his Aunt's cottage Ben sat down at the kitchen table and looked across the courtyard towards the Sail Loft. There was something about it that made him feel he was destined to be involved with it for a long time to come. He got up and opened the door that led him into the passage taking him out to the Sail Loft. Ben sat down on an old tea chest and surveyed the mess that greeted him. The first room seemed to harbour every conceivable item that you might find in ironmongers. A lot of it was covered in rust. There were very old metal containers with a variety of nails and screws, each carefully labelled and arranged by size and gauge.

It was what was hanging in the corner of the room that really caught his eye. There were two spoked wheels and a motorbike fuel tank fixed to the wall by nails and string, each with cobwebs dangling in all directions. He pushed aside other large pieces of metal and tried to reach them.

Ben wiped his hand across the fuel tank to clear away the cobwebs. This revealed the faint outline of some letters beneath the dust. He could make out a "V" and an "N" but the surface was thick with hardened oil combined with the dust.

Ben looked around for a cloth and eventually found one

in another box marked "cleaning materials." He carefully wiped away the remaining residue to reveal the full name "Vincent." He stood back in amazement. Was this really what he thought it was? No wonder Joanna had set the price high. If this really was part of an original Vincent motorbike then certainly Joanna's estimate for the contents was very conservative.

Who would know if he was right? Who could he trust enough to explain what he thought he had found?

Ben locked up the cottage and ran down to George Barton's book shop and stumbled breathlessly over the step.

"George!" Ben shouted, "Have you got anything on motorbikes?"

"I have, yes" replied George, somewhat taken aback at this sudden intrusion into his peaceful afternoon.

"However, would you like to calm down and tell me what all the excitement is about?"

"Well, you know I'm clearing out my Aunt's place?"

"Yes, that's not news though is it?" replied George sarcastically.

"No George, it isn't, but what I've found there is. That's why I need to see a book on motorbikes. Not new ones but vintage ones. Can you help me?"

"Why this sudden interest? You're usually into art and pottery books."

"I know but I've found some motorbike parts in the Sail Loft and I'd like to identify them.

"O.K. let's see what I've got I've put most of the transport books at the back of the shop"

George led Ben through tightly packed shelves of antiquarian books into the conservatory at the back.

"Here we are. These shelves are road transport. There's a chair over there. Sit down and have a browse. I'll see you later."

"Thanks George. I'll give you a shout if I find anything."

Ben scanned the shelves for anything that might hold a clue to what he needed. There were numerous biographies of riders, both international and unknown. He flicked through them, but couldn't find anything that looked like what he had found. Then just as he had decided to give up, there, jammed between two 'Motorcycle Annuals' was a small brown book with gold lettering entitled 'Vincents – The Story.' He pulled it out and made his way back to the front of the shop and George.

"Look, I've found just what I want. How much George?"

"Haven't you looked inside the cover?"

"No, I don't want to open it until I get home. How much George?" he asked excitedly.

"Well, it's eight pounds, five to you Ben."

"Thanks George," Ben replied, thrusting a five pound note in George's hand. "See you later. I'll let you know the outcome."

"Thank you Ben. Bye."

Ben didn't catch the end of George's sentence as he had already left the shop and was hurrying along the road to his cottage.

As he passed 'The Ship', he stopped, and quite out of character, decided he'd like a drink. He retraced his steps to the entrance and went in.

"Hello Jack, glass of red wine please."

"Good grief! Whatever's come over you! You haven't been in for months, Ben."

"No, I know, but today I feel I need a drink. I think I might have something to celebrate."

"What, you won the Lottery or something?" replied Jack.

"No, nothing like that. I've been cleaning out my Aunt's place…"

"We all know that" interrupted Jack, "that's nothing special."

"Let me finish Jack, you knew my uncle really well didn't you?"

"Yes, of course I did. He used to drink in here all the time. A great expert of wines was old Tom. Why?"

"Well, did he ever talk to you about motorbikes?"

"Did he! Couldn't stop him. He used to have one of the best looking bikes around. It was old. Now, what was it called? He said he used to race it when he lived in the country. He had another one too. Never saw that out on the road though. Oh, I don't think I can remember Ben. Sorry."

"I think you've already told me enough Jack. I found some spare parts in the old sail loft and the fuel tank had "Vincent" written on it…"

"That's it Ben, that's the name," said Jack interrupting again, "I've got it now, a Vincent Black Shadow, I'm sure of it."

"Really Jack, are you certain?"

"Yes, I am. Your uncle used to take it to all the shows and give demonstration rides. He was in all the papers."

"Right Jack. Let's have another drink and I'll show you what I've just bought from George up at the bookshop."

They had another drink and whilst doing so flicked through the book. They studied the pictures, ignoring the text for the moment until settling on one page that had "Black Shadow" printed beneath it.

"There you are Jack, is that it?" asked Ben.

"Well it could be, it's quite a while since I last saw your uncle ride it."

"Why did he stop?"

"Well, he'd been on one of his demonstration rides and it was a very wet day. He took a corner too sharply and slid off the road into a ditch. He was alright, but the machine was in an awful state. It took Tom some time to get his bike back here and he vowed never to ride it again. So he dismantled it and stored it out the back and I presume that's where you found it Ben?"

"Quite right Jack. It's strange, I never knew anything about it. Well, I'll get back there now and see if what I've found matches this picture. Thanks Jack, see you later."

Ben hurried back to the Sail Loft and held the book up against the motorbike pieces he had found. The 'Vincent' lettering was the same, but really he needed to find the rest of the bike to be absolutely certain.

He let himself out of his Aunt's cottage and walked the short distance to his own place. Once there, he made himself a drink, sank into a chair and started to read the book. He must have fallen asleep, as it was getting dark when he was woken up by the phone ringing.

"Hello…"

"Hello, is that Ben Treloar?"

"Yes…"

"It's Joanna Trewick. Did you get the information I left for you on the cottage and the Sail Loft?"

"Yes, hello, I did. Where are you? I…"

He stopped in mid sentence, his heart beating rapidly. What was it about Joanna that made him feel like this?

"Hello, are you still there?"

"Yes, I'm sorry. Where did you say you were?"

"I didn't, but I'm still in Truro, will be for a while. Have you decided what to do about the cottage?"

"No I haven't. Things are slightly different. I'm not sure what to do. I need to discuss it with you."

"Well, you'll have to do that with one of my colleagues. I'm really not sure how long I'll be."

"All right, thanks. Maybe I'll see you when you get back."

"Yes, perhaps. Good luck. Bye."

Ben put the phone down. He felt empty. For some strange reason he missed Joanna. He wanted to see her again, but if what she was saying was right, that wouldn't be happening at all.

He flung open the back door and walked into the garden. This was one place where he felt really at home and at peace with himself. The scent of the early evening flowers stopped him and he bent down to get closer. This was what made life worthwhile and there was no way he was going to leave his garden. So at least one decision was made – he wasn't moving.

In that case, what should he do with his Aunt's place and the Sail Loft? Why had Joanna gone away at this crucial moment? Just as he needed to discuss everything with her.

He decided he was being silly and tried to put Joanna out of his mind by checking his kiln. He had been neglecting his pottery in favour of the arrangements for the sale of his Aunt's cottage. He tried hard to get his head round sorting his pottery, but to no avail. He had an order to put together for an exhibition in Exeter, but the impetus to actually get down to making something wasn't there.

He left his kiln room and wandered aimlessly round his garden again. In the corner, at the end, under an old apple tree he could just make out the harbour across the roof tops. The lights were on in most of the buildings which made a yellow reflection on the water.

Ben reached for the notebook he always carried in his back pocket. He took the tiny pencil from the centre pages and started writing.

Quarter to eight
The light fades
Around yellow and grey roofs
Who look down
Over the darkening
Water below
Deep green
And blue
Rippling

Boats at their moorings
Tugging
Twisting
Moaning
As the tide
Pulls them
To and fro
Blank windows
Dark to the gaze
Except one
A single light
Heralding
The evening
To come.

He replaced the pencil, closed his notebook and returned it to his pocket. He had captured that moment in time and would return to it sometime in the future. Apart from his pottery and his love of all things artistic, Ben had always enjoyed writing. Even at school he had written lengthy adventure stories, divided into chapters that filled an exercise book. It was, however, poetry he got most satisfaction from writing. It captured the moment and there was an immediacy about it that you didn't find in a story. Here in this small corner of his garden he had seen something in the early evening that had aroused a need inside him to write down what he saw.

He walked slowly across the lawn, closed the door to his pottery and went inside. The chill of the early evening soon left him as he once more sat in his chair. He picked up the motorbike book, but discarded it almost immediately. All day he had been trying to come to a decision. He felt restless and uneasy. He tried to focus on all the positives in his life and identify a starting point. Firstly, he'd decided to stay put in his own cottage. So that was a plus, but what was next? He had this feeling that he was going to be attached to his Aunt's house for a long time to come, but he didn't know why.

He spent a restless night. Normally he slept until the gulls woke him around five thirty. This night had been out of the ordinary. A lot had happened during the day and it kept repeating itself time and time again in his head. Joanna featured too, and the thoughts of her took him back to London, his old job and the long-term relationship he had left behind. Ben had covered this area many times since moving, but he still felt uneasy, as if somehow he could be dragged back and lose everything he had now.

Fortunately, by morning, Ben had cleared these thoughts from his head. Over breakfast, which he ate in the garden, he mused over his plans for the day.

Really, he should be putting his exhibition pieces together and seeing how much more he needed. Then there was his Aunts and the Sail Loft. Oh, and of course Joanna. Just where was she and why was she being so evasive? Then, why should she be anything other than the professional estate agent? There was nothing between them. She was just doing her job and sometimes that took her away.

Ben finished his breakfast, walked across the damp lawn and peered over the wall at the harbour below him. He could just make out George Barton on his bike. That could only mean one thing. He was taking his boat out.

Ben dashed back into the house, grabbed his coat, locked up and ran as fast as he could to the harbour. George Barton meanwhile, had clambered down the harbour steps and onto his boat. Ben shouted across the harbour. George waved and told him to hurry up.

As George steered the boat out of the harbour, Ben glanced back at his home and then to his Aunts. Maybe George would have an answer, after all it was he who had persuaded Ben to make the move in the first place.

George took the boat about half a mile off shore and then handed over to Ben.

"Keep her in a straight line parallel with the coast, while I find the fishing tackle. I've brought some bait so we'll go a bit further west before we stop."

Ben kept the boat on course with one eye on the coastline. "George."

"Yeah."

I've got to make my mind up about my Aunt's place."

"I thought you'd already done that."

"No, I've changed my mind, had another idea. I think in a way I've confused the issue."

"How's that then?" asked George.

"Well, I'm staying put. In my place I mean. It's all I ever wanted and I think I'd be mad to leave it so soon. In any case I can't afford to move. I haven't built up enough business through my pottery to have made anything out of it yet."

"That sounds fine to me," said George, "but what will you do with Jessie's place?"

This sounded funny coming from George as Ben never called his Aunt by her first name. Perhaps he should, after all he wasn't a child anymore.

"Well, I think I might have found something amongst all the junk that might go someway towards an idea I have," explained Ben.

"How's that then? Not something to do with that book I sold you is it?"

"Well, partly, yes George, but I've got a great deal of checking to do first."

George stopped the engine and let the boat drift. He handed Ben a rod and cast his own into the sea. They sat for some time without exchanging a word. Ben enjoyed the silence as he watched the float bobbing up and down in the water.

He was lost in his own thoughts and remembered the first time he'd been out in the boat with George. George had been an Art teacher, you could tell that by the way he dressed, and Ben had been impressed with the way in which he saw things. They'd sat in the boat and watched the sun set over Penzance. Ben had remembered it in words and could describe the changes in colour in detail. George, however, somehow repainted the whole scene before your eyes as it happened. In everything he had a different perspective from other people. Yet both he and Ben knew instantly what each other was seeing and describing. It was uncanny. One through words and the other through colour-an impression.

George had made a lifelong study of the Newlyn artists' colony and lectured all over the world during the winter months. Ben had attended some of his lectures at the local college and had been stunned by how charismatic a speaker he was. In his shop he seemed unassuming, almost reticent, but still knowledgeable about a wide variety of topics.

It was George's goading, nagging and prodding that had made up Ben's mind to move here in the end. George had made him see the benefits of a move over his own misgivings and insecurities. In a way, George had been his mentor, his key to unlocking his future.

The line jerked in Ben's hand and pulled him back to reality.

"I've got a bite George!"

"OK. Start to pull it in. Slowly, mind. You don't want to lose it."

Surprisingly he reeled the fish in quite easily. He didn't recognise it, as he was expecting a mackerel.

"Whatever's that?" he asked George.

"It's a Pollack," George replied. "It's a good size too. You'll be able to eat that later."

They carried on fishing for a further hour, but caught nothing else.

"Better get back now Ben. I've got a business to run you know."

George turned the boat around and returned to the harbour. Ben decided he didn't fancy fish and gave it to George.

Ben had enjoyed the trip out in the boat, but hadn't really resolved anything. However, the sea air made him feel hungry so he headed for Jenny's café, whilst George made his way to his shop.

"Morning Jenny, coffee and a large slab of fruit cake please."

"You're in a better mood today. What's done that?"

"I've just been out with George fishing."

"Catch anything?"

"Yeah, a pollack. I didn't fancy eating it so George has got it."

"Catch anything else or was that it?"

"No, we didn't have much luck, but it was good to be out on the water."

Ben always felt relaxed with Jenny, but then he'd known her longer than anyone else in the village. She was a bit younger than him and when he'd come down to stay with his Aunt and Uncle they'd sit on the harbour wall talking about what they were going to do with their lives.

It seemed strange to him now to see her running a café, albeit one that stayed open all year round. She was far too qualified for the job. She had left the area after she left school and went to University to study Archaeology. Everyone had thought she was mad and didn't really understand her.

She'd always been fascinated by the history of the area and had spent most of her holidays on archaeological digs all over the country. She'd written a highly praised book on the ancient sites of Cornwall, which sold very well, particularly in America.

However, she'd injured her back whilst surfing and found working on digs more difficult. So she decided to move back home to carry on her local research and writing.

It brought in steady money and when the Harbour Cafe came up for sale she had enough to buy it. She'd changed it completely from a dark unwelcoming place into a thriving business with photographs of many of the sites she'd worked on around the walls.

Jenny attracted visitors from miles around and some from abroad who had read her book. Ben was pleased to see she had done so well, as he knew she was in pain from her back most days.

"What are you dreaming of today Ben?" asked Jenny as she sat down opposite him.

"Well, funnily enough, you and this Café."

"Are you now? Whatever interest could I have for you, let alone the café?"

"I was just thinking how well you've done here. It's the ideal spot to sit and watch the world go by. Don't you miss something more academic than this?"

"No, not at all. I still do my walks and research. I'm working on another book you know, all about standing stones."

"You kept that quiet, Jenny. Do you remember those days as children sitting on the harbour wall?"

"I do. Planning our futures weren't we? Well, we haven't done so badly have we?"

"No, I think you've done remarkably well and keeping this place open all year round takes a lot of doing."

"You're right. It is hard work, but having the restaurant open in the evening is what really makes the money. I suppose it helps being well known too, people come to look at you."

"Can I ask you something personal Jenny?"

"Go on then, but I know what you're going to say - why didn't I ever get married."

"Yes, exactly. You always said you'd be married young and have loads of children like your mum."

"I know, but then my career took over and I never really

met anyone special. You did though, didn't you?"

"How did you know that?"

"It was very easy. When you came to your Uncle's funeral, and we all came back here after, someone's name kept coming up every time you opened your mouth. You didn't notice, but we all thought it was really funny. It quite cheered us up, on what was really a sad day."

"Oh dear, was I that obvious?"

"Yes, I'm afraid you were. Is it because of her you moved down here? To get away?"

"Partly, yes. We'd been very close for some time and had planned to be together permanently one day."

"What went wrong?"

"Usual story really. She was with me, but seeing someone else at the same time. I couldn't believe it when I found out. I tried to understand why and put everything right, but she didn't want to know. Wouldn't even discuss it with me. So I thought, right that's it. I'm off to do my own thing, to be free from everything. To carve out a new life. It was very hard though, because despite what she's done I still feel the same about her and that won't ever change."

"You don't know that. You might meet someone down here. I understand how you must feel, but you've got to move on. Be positive. I had to be over my back didn't I?"

"Yes Jenny, you did and you've succeeded, but then you were always more positive than me. I tend to look on the dark side, as if everything's going to go wrong."

"Well it's about time we changed you and got you out of it. Come on, take me up to your house. I want to see the pottery you're making for this exhibition."

"What about the café, you can't just leave it?"

"Course I can, Sam will take over, wont you?" She shouted at the kitchen. A somewhat muffled voice replied that they would cope quite well.

Jenny was really interested in Ben's work and spent some time talking to him about his pottery. It was years since they'd spoken together for this long and Ben felt at ease. He also realised that Jenny hadn't been in his house either, so he showed her round, apologising for the state of everything as they went, to such an extent, that Jenny told him in no uncertain manner to shut up!

He did eventually. They ended up eating sandwiches in the garden talking once again about their future plans. Jenny seemed to be so certain about everything, but Ben still couldn't get his head round what he wanted to do.

They went on like this most of the afternoon, until in the end they walked down to the harbour and sat on the wall.

"There you are Ben, back where we started twenty years ago."

"Thanks a lot Jenny, it's been great talking to you again."

"I must get back to the café, they'll wonder where I am. See you soon Ben – make a definite decision. I had to."

"I will Jenny. Bye."

"Bye."

He watched her walk up the road to her café, with her auburn hair trailing behind her as it was caught by the wind. He'd forgotten just how nice she was and so intuitive.

Now he must get back to sorting out his Aunt's cottage. Immediately he thought of Joanna and those eyes. He wondered if she was back yet. He'd go and phone and see, but then what if she wasn't there. What would he say? He thought better of it and walked to his Aunt's.

He went straight to the Sail Loft, sat on an old dusty chair and looked around. On the wall were the motorbike parts, but where was the rest? Ben moved an old shelf unit and found a box full of old tools underneath. Next to that a roll of carpet tied with very thick hairy string that cut into his hands. Already he was covered in dust and oil from some of the tools. He moved another box which contained rolls of electric cable and wire, plugs, junction boxes and fuses.

Each box he opened contained similar items. No bike parts here he thought. After Ben had moved rolls of wallpaper, two window frames and countless jam jars, holding different sized screws and nails, he stopped. He was getting nowhere. He had to do this more systematically. He'd have to put some of the boxes in the main part of the cottage and then move through the Sail Loft room by room.

The larger items that were weatherproof he stacked carefully in the yard. The boxes of tools, jars of nails and screws and anything else to go with home repairs he piled up at one end of the first room near the door to the passage. He then took a number of smaller boxes back into the kitchen and put them on the table. These he would sort through first. At least he had made a start and consequently, felt much better about it. Ben looked at the boxes on the table. There were ten. He opened the first one. Inside he found books, carefully packed with some looking as if they'd never been read. There were novels by people he'd never heard of, leather bound copies of collections of poems and guide books to obscure places abroad. Each box yielded something new and different. Ben was surprised how clean and dust free the books were considering where they'd been kept. His eyes darted from one title to another. He was fascinated by the diversity of subject matter and of authors.

He'd soon unpacked all ten boxes leaving the kitchen with piles of books all over the floor. Ben had tried to sort them as he'd gone along. He glanced across the room and noted that volumes by Dickens and Hardy were running neck and neck with each other.

He'd particularly noticed a collection of poems with gold lettering on a dark green soft leather background. He'd opened it to see an inscription inside.

"To Jess, love Tom. May 1948."

If his Aunt didn't want it as a keepsake, he certainly would keep it, at his cottage amongst his own book collection.

Ben spent some time looking through the books for further inscriptions as he was determined to keep anything that had links to his family. Any other books, he thought, he would offer to George.

It was whilst he was sitting on the kitchen floor, opening and shutting book covers looking for inscriptions, that Ben began to formulate an idea for the Sail Loft and the cottage. When he was teaching, Ben had often spent the long summer holidays with his Great Aunt in Dorset. There he had enjoyed visiting local markets mainly looking for old books, but sometimes finding interesting pieces of pottery too.

At one of these markets, he couldn't remember which: it might have been Dorchester, but then it could have been Bridport: he had discovered a pottery shop with a café at the back...

He would spend time looking at the pottery for ideas rather than buying, before going through to the back for a coffee. Ben would sit at a table reading a book he had just bought on the market and listen to the conversations going on around him. He once plucked up enough courage to ask an elderly couple what they thought of the café. They told him how much they enjoyed coming there, because you could look at the pottery at the same time. What if there were books rather than pottery he had asked them too. They had hesitated, enquired if they were old or new books and then hesitated again, looking rather bewildered.

Ben put it another way. If there was a second hand bookshop that had a café attached to it or even actually part of it, would they sit and look at books while they were drinking their coffee. They had agreed that that was an interesting idea, particularly if there were comfortable chairs or even settees. A more casual approach.

Ben had carried this idea with him ever since and had told many friends about it. They had all laughed and said he'd never do it. There was one big snag to all this though, Ben had no business experience and certainly wouldn't know where to start.

Even if this was what he should do, he immediately put obstacles in the way. Firstly there was George. He sold books and antiques. He wouldn't like the competition from another book shop. Secondly, there was Jenny with the Harbour Café and Restaurant. She would be in competition too. Thirdly, there was his Aunt and the sale of her cottage. Lastly, there was the money. How could he possibly finance such a venture?

Ben picked up the phone and dialled the Estate Agent. He asked for Joanna, but was told again that she was away on business. He asked that they put the sale of his Aunt's cottage on hold and he would contact them again when he was ready. This they said they were quite happy to do.

Ben spent the next few days attempting to make a clear plan of what he would do. He didn't really want to talk to anyone until he had formulated what was right in his own mind. To this end he sank himself into his work and avoided all contact with Jenny, George or the Estate Agents. His Aunt Jess, however, was a different matter. It was her cottage and ultimately she would have the final say. Perhaps he should talk to her first then at least he'd know where he was. He didn't. Instead he spent hours in his pottery preparing for the exhibition in Exeter.

For some reason he felt more confident with his designs and he experimented with glazes. He produced some very different pieces from usual and was not at all sure he liked the change. Maybe if he left them for a few days and came back to them, he'd see them in a new light.

Ben did just that. The next few days were quite wonderful, mainly because he was working and not spending much time

socialising or worrying about the outcome of the Sail Loft. He
did do some thinking, but only on a superficial level. He really
did, for once, let himself become totally engrossed in his pottery.
It was so therapeutic and calming, as it always had been right
from when he began, whilst teacher training.

When he started, his style had been quite a joke amongst
his fellow students. Every pot he made appeared to lean to one
side. It had taken him months to produce the first upright pot.
A piece he had treasured ever since and which now stood
proudly on his window sill. A reminder, if ever he needed one,
of where he had started and to keep his feet firmly on the ground
whenever success came his way.

He had now almost produced enough exhibition pieces.
Ben had developed, over the years, an interest in sculpture and
always liked to include one or two examples in any exhibition
work he undertook.

This time was no exception. He was working on three pieces
based on interlocking hands. He had tried something similar
soon after leaving college, but had not been very successful.
Now, as he had more experience and had a particular style of
his own, he felt more confident about making the idea work
for him.

So his target was to finish these three sculptures, put the
exhibition together and pack it off to Exeter. He always liked
to send everything on ahead rather than risk taking it in his car,
which was old and rather unreliable. He preferred to travel by
train anyway as he found it more relaxing and he always got a
buzz out of crossing the River Tamar via Brunel's Saltash bridge.

So it was that, a week later, Ben stood outside his cottage
watching his exhibition pieces being driven away to Exeter. He
decided against walking down to the harbour for a drink and
went back inside to start packing. He always stayed in the same
place when he went to Exeter. A B&B near the station, which
was comfortable but you did have to be tolerant of the trains.

He didn't mind them at all, but sometimes they could keep you awake at night.

His journey to Exeter had been quite uneventful and he had enjoyed the crossing over the Tamar denoting the change from Cornwall into England!

After unpacking, he'd walked into town to where his pottery was to be exhibited. There was a poster in the art gallery window with his name in the middle of a list of exhibitors. He went into see where his pots were set out. He was impressed. They'd been laid out against a perfect neutral background which showed them at their best.

He had a quick word with the gallery owner about arrangements for the opening before leaving.

The opening was more glamorous than usual with local dignitaries present who insisted on making speeches, each trying to better the other. Eventually they stopped and everyone could relax over a glass of wine and do what they'd come for-look at the exhibits.

"Hello Ben," a voice he recognised spoke behind him.

He swung round. It was Joanna. His eyes met hers and he was lost.

"Hello Joanna, how are you? What are you doing here?"

"Same as many other people I expect. I read about it in the local paper, saw your name and here I am."

"It's really good to see you. I thought you'd disappeared for good."

"No, but quite often I'm away for months on business. I always seem to get the difficult sales."

"I hope mine's not in that category."

"No, of course not. Have you decided what to do yet?"

"I have, but look, you're here to see the exhibition. Would you like me to show you round?"

"Yes please. I'd like that."

They spent the next hour or so wandering round the

exhibits and chatting idly about pottery, art and sculpture.

"Are you here for long Ben?" asked Joanna.

"Only while the exhibition is on. I'm staying in a B&B down by the station. I'm probably going back the day before it finishes.

"What about your pottery?"

"Well. What's sold stays and the rest is packed and sent back to me. Sometimes there are commissions too. If that's the case I shall be busy for quite a while. Hopefully that'll be the outcome."

"So this exhibition is really important to you then?"

"Exactly - very, but then they all are. It's how I make my living. If I'm really lucky a large chain of shops may see my work and that could lead to long term commission. That would be best for me, but it'll mean a lot of hard work and not much lazing around at home!"

"I hardly think you do that. You always seem very busy to me, particularly at your Aunt's cottage."

"Yes, well that's different and hardly a job. In some ways it's actually quite relaxing. If only I could make up my mind more quickly."

"Yes, you were saying earlier that you had decided what to do."

"I have, but I have other people to consider first. The idea I have in my head is only possible if I don't affect other businesses in the village."

"I see, so this decision you've made has something to do with a scheme you've thought up for your Aunt's?"

"Yes, but at the moment it's in its early stages. I've decided to stay where I am living and hopefully develop my Aunt's place."

"That sounds intriguing. You're not going to tell me any more are you?"

"No, I'm not. Not until I'm certain what I'm doing, then

you never know, I might just ask your advice!"

Joanna said nothing more. She glared at him, smiled and winked as if she knew what he was planning. She pushed her hair back off her face and the light caught her eyes. They sparkled as she turned her head and glanced at him again. He was lost, swept away by the sensuousness of it all.

"You on for a meal tonight, Ben?" She suddenly asked. "I know a good Italian restaurant not far from here."

Ben was so taken aback by this he didn't know what to say.

"But then, if you're busy, some other time?"

"No, that's fine, I'd love to. I haven't any other plans for tonight."

Ben wished he hadn't said it like that. It wasn't how he meant it to sound at all.

"Right, I'll meet you here when the Gallery closes. Six thirty isn't it?"

"Yes Joanna. I'll see you then. Thanks, I mean I'll look forward to it. Bye."

She was gone again with a smile, a flick of the hair and the most exciting eyes he knew.

He spent the afternoon talking to other exhibitors and much to his surprise receiving complimentary remarks about his work. He'd never been very good at accepting praise and wasn't quite sure how to handle it. They seemed very impressed by his new glazes and thought he was quite daring to change from his usual style. He'd already received one commission and one sculpture and five other items had been sold. Not a bad start at all.

The latter part of the day dragged. The number of visitors dwindled and Ben found himself watching the clock awaiting Joanna's return. He couldn't wait to see those eyes again, the long dark hair and tall slim figure. He still didn't know whether she was interested in him personally or just through the link with his Aunt's cottage. Maybe he would find that out over the meal if Joanna turned up. After all, she did have a habit of disappearing.

It was nearly six thirty! He felt his heart thumping and he was nervous with anticipation, fidgeting about trying to look busy.

Then a tapping on the door. It was her. Ben opened the door, said goodnight to the Gallery owner and greeted Joanna.

"Hi, you look terrific!" he said enthusiastically.

"You don't look bad yourself even if you are still in the same clothes as this morning. And you haven't shaved!"

"That's not fair. I've only just finished here, you know that!"

"I know, I'm only kidding. Come on, it's starting to rain. Let's eat."

Joanna linked arms and almost marched Ben off down the road. They didn't speak again until they had reached the restaurant and had gone inside.

"Table for two in the name of Trewick," Joanna announced very forcefully.

"Yes Madam, this way please."

They both followed and were shown to a window table that overlooked the Cathedral. It was floodlit and the shadows of the trees nearby lined up like soldiers on sentry duty across its front.

"Good spot, eh?" asked Joanna reading his mind.

"Yes, great. Would you like a drink?"

"Sure, I'll have a red wine, and you?"

"I think I'll have the same, I don't usually drink very much."

Ben wished he hadn't said that and tried to explain that he wasn't a big drinker, but Joanna didn't seem to mind.

"Now Ben, tell me about your plans for the cottage and the Sail Loft."

"I told you earlier today that I wasn't going to discuss it with you until I was absolutely certain."

"Not even a clue?"

"No! Now tell me what you're doing here."

"All right. Well, we've been trying to sell some warehouses down by the river. We plan to convert them into flats. The problem is it's in the conservation area and the Architects are having difficulty having the plans approved."

"So what part do you play in all of this?"

"At the moment I seem to be the link between everyone who's involved, trying to reach an agreement."

"Isn't that quite a responsibility? It sounds as if you could make or break the scheme."

"Not really. Other people do all the hard work, I just see fair play!"

Their drinks arrived and they ordered the food. Joanna talked more about her job until the food was served. They talked about his exhibition whilst they ate and about life back in Penzance. Seeing Joanna here away from where she usually worked made her appear more business like and self confident.

Ben sat mesmerised by Joanna as she talked. He watched her every movement, the way her lips moved, how her nose wrinkled and in her speech the very slight lisp. He liked that, he'd always been attracted by a slight lisp. He thought it was sexy. Joanna was sexy or did he mean attractive or was it stunning, no it was more than that, she was absolutely beautiful in every way. It was the eyes though that really captivated him that drew him to her. Each time she looked at him his stomach turned over and knotted up. A strange feeling swept over him. It was something he'd never felt before. Was this what love felt like? He'd been in love before, it was part of the reason he'd moved, but this was different, very different. These were feelings he'd never experienced, so was this really true love, the one really important love everyone hopes they'll meet?

"Where have you gone, Ben?" You've hardly said a word, are you all right?"

"Yes I'm fine. I was listening to what you were saying. No, look, I've got to say that, well I, you see, Joanna…"

"Yes, what is it?"

"You know I love you don't you?"

Joanna looked him straight in the eyes and smiled. She put out her hand and squeezed his, but said nothing. They sat looking at each other for a moment holding hands across the table. Ben looked in Joanna's eyes and was sure he detected a small tear. She smiled again and said very quietly.

"I know."

She pulled back her hand, wiped the tear from her eye and spoke again.

"Shall we have coffee?"

"Yes, fine, of course."

Ben didn't know what to say. He looked at her again and she smiled such a smile that it took his breath away.

"I do mean it Joanna. I've known since I first saw you. You really are quite special."

Joanna put her finger on his lips, smiled again and then picked up her coffee, sipped it and fixed him with a glance across the top of the cup that sent a shiver down his spine.

"Come on Ben, let's go. We've got a busy day tomorrow. The meal was lovely, thank you, even if I did book it myself."

She grinned again, they rose from the table, paid and left. She linked arms with him again as if it was the most natural thing to do. They walked towards the Cathedral. He looked down at her and her up at him. They stopped. Ben pulled her towards him and their lips met, only briefly but long enough for Ben to be swept away completely. He was certain that this was a very important moment in his life.

"Come on Ben, I'll drive you home."

It was still raining so they ran across the square to where Joanna's car was parked. It took five minutes to drive Ben home. He kissed her on the cheek, thanked her for a lovely evening, got out of the car and stood in the rain as Joanna drove away.

Ben turned and felt as though he was floating towards the front door on a tide of emotion. He soon got inside, went to his room and flopped on the bed. There was a silly grin on his face like a naughty school boy. Was this what love felt like, had he at last found what he'd always been looking for? Only one thing bothered him though. Joanna hadn't actually said she loved him. She had just smiled, but what a smile.

Ben didn't see Joanna again that week. The exhibition was a great success and brought him so much work, he wasn't sure how he'd be able to keep up with it. The fact that Joanna hadn't appeared again didn't surprise him, but he did miss her and wondered where she was. He phoned the Estate Agent's in Exeter and was told quite curtly that she was out "on site". If he'd had time Ben would have walked down to the warehouses and found her, but he didn't.

On the last day of the exhibition Ben picked up what was left, picked up a long list of orders and received payment for items sold. He was in profit and had actually made something out of the sales. So with the money from the orders he should be able to put aside a little towards the Sail Loft.

Ben returned to the B&B to pick up his belongings after having seen off the remainder of his exhibition on the delivery lorry.

He bought an evening paper at the station and caught the train which for once was on time. He watched out of the window as the lights of Exeter gradually faded into the night and started to read the paper.

Most of the news was about the happenings in the villages around Exeter or students tying themselves to lamp posts to raise money. He found the Arts page and tucked away at the bottom was a short article about the exhibition. He scanned it quickly and read to himself:

"Ben Treloar's outstanding craftsmanship allied to unusual use of experimental glazes."

And then it went on to describe other artists' work. It hadn't said a lot but at least he'd been mentioned and that might generate some interest in his work.

He turned the page to reach the middle of the paper and there staring back at him was Joanna. The headline said it all. She had obviously succeeded with the sale of the warehousing. She and three men were standing next to an old crane shaking hands and as usual the smile on her face was electric.

Ben read some of the article until he became bored. It was all about the business side of the deal and that didn't interest him at all. He looked back at the picture and Joanna's lovely face and beautiful figure. Then he let his eyes drop to the bottom of the picture and the caption. There was her name clearly printed – Joanna Trewick (head of sales), then two names which meant nothing to him, but the final one made him go cold – James Trewick. He didn't stop to read what he did. Ben put the paper down and stared out of the window at the darkening sky.

Realisation hit him. It must be her husband, but when he'd seen Joanna she didn't wear a ring or was she just having him on, playing a game. He felt dreadful, absolutely devastated. He got up and went to the restaurant car to buy a drink. Once there he purchased a glass of red wine and proceeded to pace up and down the carriage not wanting to settle for a moment.

Ben felt such a fool. He kept thinking of what he'd said to Joanna during and after their meal together. She'd even kissed him and held his hand and of course that look in her eye that seemed to affect him so much.

He walked back to his seat and re-read the caption. It still read exactly the same. By the time the train had reached Plymouth he was thoroughly fed up and felt utterly helpless. There was nothing he could do whilst on the train, so he thought he'd try and sleep the rest of the way. He couldn't. So he decided to read the article about the sale of the warehouses in more detail. He learned nothing new, but one good thing did come out of it. He fell asleep. So much so that when the train reached Penzance he had to be woken by the cleaners, as everyone else had got off.

He stood outside the station hoping to catch a bus. There wasn't one. He'd just missed it. The moon was out and he could hear the boats bobbing about in the harbour as he started to walk home. It was three miles and he thought it would do him good. Thinking time and planning what to do next.

As he walked along the front past the old swimming pool, Joanna was firmly set in his mind. Maybe it was a misprint and they'd inadvertently put her surname in twice. Ideas like that kept flashing through his mind.

When he reached Newlyn the fishing boats were landing their catch, so he stopped to watch. That, at least, got his mind off Joanna for a while.

He leant against the door of one of the sheds and watched intently as the catch was unloaded, noticing the blocks of ice haphazardly thrown on top. Labels were hurriedly stuck on each box and the boxes pushed into the centre of the shed and stacked according to type. Buying started almost immediately as the fish were to be transported all over England during the night.

Ben, still quite engrossed in what was going on, became aware of a figure standing next to him.

"Hi Ben, what are you doing here, surely not buying you?"

It was Jenny. Was he glad to see a familiar face.

"Hi, I'm on my way home from Exeter. No buses so I decided to walk. Got this far and thought I'd see what was going on. Why are you here?"

"I'm buying for the Restaurant. Sam's out there bidding,

he's the expert. Ex-fisherman and chef. The ideal person. I come down every week, same day, very boring!"

"No, I'm fascinated. I've not had time to stop before, it's really a different world. The language, the speed of the sale, its all very interesting."

"How are you getting back from here Ben? Still walking?"

"Yes, I needed some time to think. It's been a strange week."

"I'll give you a lift if you like, I'm going past your cottage anyway. You look worn out. Come on, Sam will be here a while yet and he's got the van. Coming?"

"O.K. You're right. Now I've stopped walking I do feel tired and this bag is heavy."

They walked to Jenny's car with Jenny telling Ben what fish she was buying and what she was going to do with it.

They drove up the hill away from the fish market and Ben glanced across the bay at the lights in Penzance.

"How did the exhibition go Ben?" Jenny asked.

"Very well. I've sold almost everything and have a number of orders that'll keep me going for months. They particularly liked the new glazes I'd tried so I shall persevere with those for a while."

"That's really good. I'm pleased Ben. You've now got the recognition you've always deserved. Will you make me something for the café?"

"Of course I will. Suitable for the café or the restaurant, which would you prefer?"

"I think the café, then it can be seen all day by everyone. Thanks Ben, I'll pay you of course."

"No you won't. I've known you long enough to make you something because I want to, not because I have to."

Jenny dropped him off outside his cottage, said goodnight and drove off. Ben watched her go and then turned the key in the door. It was warm inside and it was only then as he took the paper from his coat pocket, that he remembered Joanna.

He looked at the picture again, at Joanna and then at who he presumed to be her husband. His stomach knotted up as he thought of her and what he'd said in the restaurant. Now he was at home, it seemed almost like a dream, but he had the photograph in front of him and in that Joanna was real enough. He put the paper down and decided to go to bed. Maybe things would be clearer in the morning.

They weren't. Ben had woken several times in the night with the same feeling in his stomach, sweating heavily and in a complete state of desperation. He kept telling himself he was being silly, after all he hardly knew Joanna and had moved very quickly to tell her how he felt. The more the words went round his head, the more he wished he hadn't said them in the first place. Joanna was married, what a fool she must think Ben is.

These thoughts wouldn't go away. Each time he woke, they were there, nagging away, covering him in total confusion. The morning wasn't any better. He'd woken early, felt awful, didn't want any breakfast and decided to go out. He flung on some old clothes, slammed the door and walked out into the damp, misty morning air.

He walked away from his village up the hill that led to the back road into Newlyn. He pulled his jacket tight round his chest, as the cold air bit into him. It was a long climb which he found a trial as he hadn't really woken up properly. At the top he reached the church and for some reason walked into the graveyard. The grass was long and wet under his feet and soon both his shoes and socks were soaked.

Ben read some of the inscriptions but didn't take in what they said. What did catch his eye though were glass domed containers that covered sculpted flowers, joined hands, doves and miniature prayer books. These intrigued him particularly as he enjoyed sculpting clay. He hadn't seen anything like this, anywhere before. Some of them were quite old and unfortunately broken, but most were in very good condition.

He walked on to see if there were any more. The sun came out and he felt warmer, as steam rose from the damp ground beneath his feet. Ben reached the far end of the graveyard, where there stood a stone carved into the shape of an artist's palette and brush. The inscription was barely readable, but he recognised the name as being that of one of the Newlyn artists' colony at the turn of the century.

He leant on an old iron gate that hung between two stone walls marking the edge of the graveyard and looked back the way he had come. The sun was catching the tops of the glass containers and the path resembled an airport landing strip with lights either side.

Ben took in the sight and the feel of the place. It had become very atmospheric. He wanted to capture that moment and remember it, to keep it in his mind and use it again one day, maybe.

He felt for the notebook and pencil he always carried with him. It was still in his pocket where he'd left it. He took it out, turned to the next blank page and wrote:

The silence
Is deafening
Warmth surrounds
The stone slabs
Standing erect
For countless years
Greys and browns
Ivy covered
Grass engulfed
Symbols
Words unheard
Some indistinguishable

The Sail Loft

There lie
Those souls
Who once
Populated
The area
Local names
Some famous
Some tragic
But all links
To our past
Through
Meaningful
Purposeful
Lives
Now silent
In their small
Piece of this
Land
No more
Worry
Happiness
Romance
Or fun
Gone physically
But
Through
Name
Alone
Linked forever
to
the future

Ben closed the notebook and returned it and the pencil to his pocket.

"Right. I'll see you later. I must get back to the office. They'll wonder where I am. Thanks for the coffee. Till tonight then."

Ben let her out and returned to his list of orders. He spent the rest of the day sorting out how much clay he'd need and mixing more glaze. Whilst doing that he went over what Joanna had said and tried to get his own feelings into perspective.

He was none the wiser when he left in the evening and caught the bus into Penzance. He'd already decided that whatever time he left Joanna's he would walk home, as he'd so enjoyed it the night before.

Her flat was quite easy to find as the new quay development was very close to the bus station. Needless to say, she had a penthouse suite that had panoramic views over Mounts Bay.

She looked stunning. Her hair was up, which made her look slimmer in the face and she was wearing a tight, but very flattering black dress. As usual, it was her eyes that attracted him most of all. They sparkled and shone in the subdued light and almost flashed as she spoke. He noticed the slight lisp again. Another attractive feature of her character.

His eyes eventually left hers and looked around the room… Joanna had been talking to him and telling him where everything was, but he wasn't taking it in. He was just looking at her, the way she moved, the way she spoke and especially the way she looked. Absolutely terrific.

"…and out here…wake up Ben!…on the balcony you can see for miles."

Ben followed the skyline. It was a clear night and the stars were sparkling, just like Joanna's eyes. He turned and looked at her. She returned his glance.

"Shall we eat now? It's just about ready."

"Yes, thanks. You've a lovely place here Joanna, the view is wonderful."

"I like sitting out here at night, particularly in the summer, to watch the sunset. You've never seen so many colours and the light is so clear. It's no wonder so many painters want to live down here. Do you like chilli?"

"Yes I do."

"Good, because that's what I've made. Can you open the wine please? I thought red would be best with this. Is that all right with you?"

"Yes fine" Ben replied. It was so long since anyone had cooked a meal for him he didn't really know what to say, apart from agreeing to everything!

The meal was delicious. Joanna was certainly a good cook. They talked about her flat, how long she'd been there and about his exhibition and her job in Exeter. It all seemed rather mundane to Ben after the spontaneity of the restaurant in Exeter. There now seemed to be a distance between them. Why had she asked him round? Was it another impulse or was she genuinely interested in him? Or perhaps she just wanted his company because she was at a loose end.

"You look really gorgeous tonight Joanna," Ben broke the silence. I like the dress and you look different with your hair up."

"Thank you Ben. You look good too. It's the first time I've seen you not wearing jeans."

"I never was a great one for dressing up. I never liked having to wear a tie when I was teaching, let alone a suit. So now I slob around I suppose, but casually."

"Look, when we were in Exeter."

"Yes."

"I heard what you said Ben. I think I understand how you feel, but you've got to give me time and space. I'm in a bit of a void emotionally. I don't really know what I want at the moment. Do you understand?"

"Yes I think so, but then I can't change how I feel, not just like that."

"No I know you can't and I do appreciate what you're saying."

With that Joanna got up, grabbed Ben by the hand and led him back out onto the balcony.

"Now look up at those stars Ben. There's one for everyone up there. Look, there's yours and there's mine, right close together."

She looked up at him and smiled. Ben took her face in his hands and gently kissed the end of her nose. She laughed, but came closer. Ben dropped his arms round her waist, leant forward and met her lips with his. A shiver ran down his spine as they kissed.

Joanna's arms moved slowly round his waist and up his back and she pulled him closer. This was beyond his wildest dream. It was what he'd wanted for so long.

They both opened their eyes together, stood back and smiled.

"I do love you Joanna."

"I know Ben, it's good being together like this."

She pulled him close again, wiped the lipstick away from his cheek and gave him another kiss. Ben was in heaven. They sat out on the balcony holding hands and talking till well after midnight. The stars still shone and Ben felt content and happy for the first time since he'd moved to the area.

"Have you got to get back tonight Ben?" Joanna suddenly asked.

"Well, I had intended on walking back via the Newlyn fish market, but that can wait. No, I don't."

"That was a long winded answer to get to no!"

"Why do you ask?"

"I thought you might like to stay here with me tonight. Would you Ben or am I being forward?"

"No Joanna, I'd love to stay. It's just not what I'd expected, not after the newspaper article."

"I told you, that's over. Come here you silly thing."

Joanna pulled him towards her almost dragging him out of his chair and plonked another huge kiss on his lips. The shivers went down his spine again and he was swept away.

The morning was a rush. They woke up late as Joanna had forgotten to set her alarm.

"Hurry up Ben, I'm late for work."

"You've only got to walk round the corner."

"Yes I know, but I've got to see a client in ten minutes."

With that, Ben stuffed his feet into his shoes, grabbed his coat and followed Joanna out of the door. They held hands down the stairs, kissed at the outside door and went their separate ways, with Ben still clutching a piece of toast. He ate it as he waited for the bus home.

"Morning Ben, been into town already? You must have been up early or have you been watching the fish sales again?"

It was Jenny. She'd spotted him getting off the bus and couldn't resist a little wind-up.

"Oh, hello. No, I've, well really, actually, I'm on my way home. I've been out."

"I can see that and by the look of you, you've been out all night. Come on Ben, you can't pull the wool over my eyes. I've known you too long."

"Yes you're right Jenny, I stayed with friends, up late, tired, must go, see you later."

"Bye Ben. See you."

Jenny watched him wander up the road to his cottage with a puzzled look on her face. What friends in town? He hadn't any as far as she knew.

Ben made himself some more breakfast when he got in, which he ate quickly, grabbed a cup of coffee and sat in a chair. There he thought back over the last twenty four hours and all that had happened. Joanna had been wonderful, but how serious was she? Maybe she was lonely without her husband and just wanted some company. He just couldn't seem to get his head round what she was at, at all. Trust Jenny to be there when he got back. Still she won't know where he's really been and who with.

With these thoughts in his mind it wasn't long before Ben dropped off to sleep. He didn't wake until mid-afternoon, had a shower and decided once dressed he'd go for a walk round the harbour. He felt like some fresh air and maybe even a cup of coffee in Jenny's café. He wanted to see if she was still inquisitive about where he had been.

He walked down the steps at the end of the harbour wall and onto the rocks at the bottom. The tide was out so he kept clambering over the seaweed strewn surface until he reached the water's edge. There he found a flat rock to sit on took off his trainers and dangled his feet in the sea. He pulled them out again pretty quickly as the water was freezing. Gradually he let them in again. First his toes, then he slid the rest of his foot under surface. Both feet were now submerged. He leant back on his arms and let the sun catch his face. He felt the warmth and could almost feel the power put energy back into his tired body.

It was quiet, but for the sea lapping against the base of the rock below him. Gulls wheeled overhead, but made little noise, unlike their performance at five in the morning. Ben felt relaxed. This was what he'd moved here for. Time to sit and take in what nature presented. He didn't mind if it was wet and blowing a gale or warm and sunny like today, he was at peace with himself and the natural world around him.

It was here that he could get inspiration for his pottery, see the colours for new glazes and use the natural features as designs. He'd have loved to have sat and painted what he could see right now, but wasn't as confident with his drawing as he was with clay. Sometimes he would take a sketch book out with him, but often people would want to look at what he was doing and that put him off.

So he'd find somewhere quiet, make a quick sketch, sometimes a photo as well, and then work on it back at home in his studio. He'd also make a note of colours and shapes and the light or shade. This always helped to develop what he had seen.

Ben put his hand in his pocket to take out his notebook. It wasn't there. This was the first time he'd been without it. He tried every pocket in turn. He began to panic. His every thought was in that book. His poetry, notes about glazes, drawings, designs for pots, everything.

He sat for a moment or two. Had he taken it in to Joanna's? No, different coat. So he hadn't left it there. Had he put it in his back pocket? He sometimes did that. He was baffled.

Ben put his trainers back on without drying his feet and walked back across the rocks to the harbour wall. As he walked through the village he stuck his head in George's shop.

"You all right George?"

"Oh hello Ben. Haven't seen you for a few days. I'm going out in the boat when the tide's up a bit. Fancy coming?"

"Yes I'd love to. What time?"

"About six. That all right with you?"

"Yes fine. I'll see you then. Bye."

"Bye Ben."

Ben walked past the pub round by the bus stop and up to Jenny's café. He opened the door and walked in. It was packed out. So he walked past the counter and out through the passage into the back garden. Out in the garden there were six or seven tables set on shingle bases each surrounded by scented flowers and bushes. It was a walled garden and consequently very quiet and secluded. You could have been anywhere and Ben often imagined he was.

There were two or three families out there too, but they were running from table to table so he couldn't work out who was with who.

"So this is where you're hiding now is it? What a mysterious man you are today Ben."

"It was Jenny again with her auburn hair tied back and wearing huge dangly earrings.

"What on earth have you got hanging off your ears Jenny?"

"Oh, thank you very much. They're ethnic, you know, old Celtic design. Very fashionable at the moment. Don't they suit me then?"

"It's not that. They make you look top heavy, as if you're going to fall over any minute."

With that, Jenny sat down opposite him, took off the earrings and put them down heavily on the table.

"Satisfied?"

"You didn't have to do that. I was only making an observation. I didn't mean to upset you."

"You haven't. I just thought I'd wind you up again like this morning. Easy to get you going isn't it?"

"You rotten thing. Now go and get me some tea."

"Yes sir. What would sir like?"

"A cream tea, but with coffee instead of tea, please."

With that they both laughed and Jenny skipped inside to the kitchen. Ben picked up the earrings. He recognised the design and they were heavy. As Jenny returned with his cream tea he remembered where he'd seen the design. It was on the cover of one of her books.

"Here you are sir! One cream tea, I mean coffee, with two scones and loads of raspberry jam as you usually ask for it anyway."

"Thank you Jenny. I'm sorry about the earrings. They're lovely and very much like one of your book covers aren't they?"

"Spot on. I had them made especially as part of the book promotion. Sold quite a few. This is the last pair so I don't wear them very often. Now listen Ben, I've got something here for you."

Ben looked up from spreading his scone to see his notebook in Jenny's hand.

"Where on earth did you find that? I've been looking all over for it. I thought I'd lost it."

"It was on the bus this morning. Someone found it and gave it to the driver. Your name's inside and as I know you, I said I'd pass it on when I saw you next. So here you are."

"Thanks. Have you…?"

"Looked inside?" Jenny interrupted. "Only to check it was yours and I read one poem, Very good, just how the village is at night. You're very good. Not just a mad potter after all. A writer too!"

"I'm glad I've got it back. It's so useful. Whenever I have a thought or idea I jot it down. Sometimes I don't look at it again for months."

"Just as well you didn't leave it at your "friends" house isn't it? Now which friends would they be then Ben?" Jenny was winding him up again particularly as she knew full well that he had no friends in Penzance.

"Well, I've not known them long Jenny. They're new friends."

"Oh are they. Do they have names, these friends of yours?"

"Jenny, stop being so nosey."

"I'm not Ben. But you're usually so open about everything. This all sounds very mysterious."

"Well, one of them is called Joanna and…"

"Would that be Joanna Trewick, the estate agent handling the sale of your Aunt's cottage?"

"Yes, but how did you know that?"

"Ben, this is a village. I'm local, I know what's going on and your Aunt Jess told me to keep an eye on things while she's away."

"Does that include me too?"

"Yes, I suppose it does, but only where you're Aunt's

interests are concerned. Your private life is your own."

"Oh is it? You wouldn't think so the way you interrogate me."

"I like you really Ben! Must dash. I've got work to do. See you later."

In a way, Jenny knew him too well, even though their lives had taken completely different directions. He enjoyed his cream tea whilst he read through his notebook. He doodled on a plain page and made a few outline designs for pots. He looked round the garden at some of the flower pots and the shadows they cast across the path. There were climbing roses, fragrant ones, and a fragrance that hung in the air. This garden was so peaceful and the complications of the work outside seemed a million miles away. He didn't really want to leave, but knew he really ought to be getting on with his pottery orders.

As he finished his coffee, he noticed that Jenny was there again, clearing up the tables. Ben watched her as she moved from table to table. He'd not really looked at her much before, mainly, he thought because they'd known each other for so long. He'd not been there when she was growing up and making a name for herself, but they were similar ages and there was something that had always attracted him to her. Even when they were younger. She was easy to talk to and always had been and despite all her success she was still the same.

"Now what are you staring at Ben? You could always give me a hand you know."

"Sorry, I was miles away. Of course I'll help. Have you been busy all day?"

"Yes, but then you get days like that and it is good for business."

"When you've cleared all this do you get much of a break before you start serving in the restaurant?"

"Sometimes, like today for instance. We've taken some bookings, but they're not until later so while chef gets organised

I can have a break. So where are you taking me then Ben?!!"

"Oh, I hadn't really..."

"It's all right, I'm joking. You're getting far too serious these days, Ben, you used to be so much fun."

"Right, that's it. Stop messing me about Jenny. Grab your coat and come with me."

"Where are we going?"

"Wait and see. It's a surprise."

Jenny quickly told her chef what to do and followed Ben out of the café.

"Hey you've gone without paying Ben," she shouted after him.

"Oh, that's all right, I know the owner."

Jenny laughed to herself as she caught him up and put her arm through his. Ben looked at her and smiled. They walked round the harbour towards the breakwater. George was already on the boat and waved at Ben.

"You both coming out with me?" He shouted up at them.

"Yes," said Ben "here you are Jenny, an early evening cruise with George and me. You can catch your own fish instead of buying it in Newlyn."

"I'm not dressed for fishing. I can't be too long, no more than an hour."

"Don't worry," said George, "if you haven't caught anything by then it wont be worth staying out there."

"All right then. Ben give me a hand please, remember my back."

Ben helped Jenny on board and sat on the engine housing behind the cabin and smiled at Ben again. He helped George cast off and they were away out of the harbour entrance.

It was choppy once they were in deeper water and spray was coming over the bows and drenching them. Jenny went inside the cabin with George while Ben cast a few lines off the side of the boat. It was now that Ben wished he hadn't just had a cream tea. With the pitch of the boat he became unsteady on his feet and kept slipping over. Jenny and George were laughing at him which didn't help matters at all.

"Come on Ben, show me how to catch a fish" shouted Jenny from the safety of the cabin."

"You come out and try then. It's harder than you think."

Jenny did just that. She sat on the engine housing again, took a rod from Ben, put her feet up on the side on the boat and reeled in a mackerel.

"There you are Ben. Easy, isn't it? Now what were you saying about how hard it is?"

That's not fair. I've had that line out there for ages."

"Yes you have, but it was me who reeled it in. Come on Ben, sit here next to me and try again. Put your feet up on the side like I did."

Ben followed her instructions and to his amazement caught a mackerel too. Between them they caught six before George took them back to the harbour.

"I must dash Ben. Bring the mackerel up the restaurant later and we'll get chef to cook them for us... You'll come too won't you George?"

"I'd love to. We'll get cleaned up here and meet you after we've had a drink."

"O.K. Bye George. Bye Ben."

"Bye Jenny thanks for the instruction!"

"My pleasure. See you later."

"Nice girl that Ben." said George, "she always has been. You could do worse you know."

"What's this you're running now George, a marriage bureau?"

"No I just thought, you two having known each other for so long and you do get on well."

"By that you mean that Jenny's always winding me up and outdoing me in just about everything."

"No I don't Ben. You know she's been through a lot with that back injury. Her whole life is that café and restaurant, she never goes out. I just thought as you've been friends a long time you ought to take her somewhere else one day. Give her a treat."

Ben thought about what George was saying before he answered. He thought of Joanna too and how he felt for her. Jenny was a long standing friend. No more than that.

"It's difficult George. I'm seeing someone else at the moment and my time's taken up with her when I'm not working on my pots."

"You mean that girl from the Estate Agents don't you?"

"Does everyone here know about her or has Jenny been spreading rumours?"

"No she hasn't, she's very loyal to you."

"So how did you know George?"

"Usual thing. You never stop talking about her and she was at the exhibition with you in Exeter."

"How did you know that?"

"I was there, but you were too busy with her to notice anyone else."

"I didn't realise. I'm sorry, were you really there?"

"Yes I was and have you looked at your sales and orders list yet?"

"No, not really, why?"

"Take a close look, you might recognise one or two local names. Come on Ben, we mustn't keep Jenny waiting. You bring the mackerel and we'll have that drink on the way."

Ben and George climbed up the steps from where they had tied up the boat and went into the Ship.

"Evening Jack," said George. "Pint and a red wine please."

"Right George. Becoming quite a regular now then Ben. Surprised you can find the time."

Jack winked at Ben as he got the drinks. Ben didn't rise to the bait and Jack said no more.

"What did you catch then?" Jack asked.

"Half a dozen mackerel. We're taking them up to Jenny's for Sam to cook."

Ben and George sat and had their drinks. They talked about fishing, about Jenny and how well she'd done and a little about Ben's plans.

"George, let me ask you something. See what you think about this as an idea."

"O.K. Is it about the motorbike again?"

"Well, indirectly. Now listen. Say I turned my Aunt's old sail loft into a pottery and had a café at the front of the cottage and let the top of the cottage out as a holiday flat."

"Yes," said George, waiting for the rest.

"Or I could have a book shop like you with a pottery too, and the cafe and the flat."

"Hang on a minute. Am I hearing this right? You want a shop like mine, a café like Jenny's, a pottery and a holiday flat all in one?"

"Yes, I suppose I do in a way, but I don't want to cut into what you and Jenny are doing. Maybe I've explained it badly."

"No, you haven't. I think I understand what you are saying. Somewhere in there is a good idea. Now, think again and start right at the beginning."

"Well, firstly, in no way do I want to affect anyone's business in the village."

"Good, that's a start." George replied with relief.

"When I was showing Joanna Trewick round to value the cottage, both she and I noticed all the boxes and bits and pieces in the Sail Loft. When I had a close look and realised what was there I looked on things in a different light. I could see the potential of developing it."

"So you thought of a shop or pottery?"

"Not to start with, that developed later. I thought I could sell what was there. Antiques, bric-a-brac, odds and ends. You know. You see you sell mainly books and a few antiques. I thought I could do the reverse."

"I understand. Where does the café come into it?"

"I was in Dorset years ago on holiday and came across this shop selling pottery. I went in just to get ideas, but then noticed a door at the back that led into a café. Whilst in there I thought of alternatives to a pottery. At the time, I was into books and writing, so I decided there and then that I would have a second hand bookshop with a café at the front. In other words, decide which book you want while you have a cup of coffee. It's been a dream of mine ever since. Now I could really do it."

"Quite a story Ben. Which option are you going to go for now?"

"That's the problem, I think I've got to sort everything out in the Sail Loft before finally deciding. Also I do not want to upset you or Jenny by doing what you have already done."

"I don't think you will. It's a big undertaking starting up a business, but you're half way there with your pottery. Healthy competition never did anyone any harm. We might all benefit, even the whole village by attracting more people. I'd go for it Ben. Come on, drink up and we'll go and see what Jenny thinks."

"Thanks George. Don't forget the mackerel."

Fortunately Jenny was able to take a break and listen to Ben's ideas. She too thought Ben should go ahead, but also suggested that all three of them ought to see what was in the Sail Loft and advise Ben on what to do.

They didn't eat until quite late as there wasn't time to prepare and cook the mackerel until after the last customers had been served. So by the time Ben and George left it was early morning.

Ben slept well and in the morning decided he would phone Joanna and tell her of his plans. He was, needless to say, unable to talk to her as she was out of the office. It was when he was told this that he realised how much she meant to him and how much he missed her. It also irritated him too. He never seemed to know where she was and she never thought to tell him. Why not? What was she hiding?

Ben decided not to go to the Sail Loft until Jenny and George could find time to meet him there. Instead he worked on his orders. George was right. Ben went through the list of sales and orders to discover how many local people had either been to the exhibition and had ordered or bought items. He was indeed very flattered by that, particularly as they'd had so far to travel to see the exhibition.

The day passed quite uneventfully but as he stopped work in the late afternoon, the phone rang.

"Hi, it's Joanna. I gather you phoned the office this morning."

"Yes I did. Are you away again?"

"I'm in Newquay. A hotel sale. How are you?"

"Fine and you?"

"Yes, great. What did you want?"

"Oh it can wait till you get back. Only an idea about the Sail Loft. I thought you might be able to help."

"Are you selling it after all then?"

"No, I want to develop it. Look, I'll tell you, as I said, when I see you."

"All right, I'll phone when I'm back and remember there's a star for everyone. Look up there tonight. You'll see us side by side. Bye bye Ben."

His mind started racing. Where was she really, who was she with? Did she want to see him again?

Perhaps it was just that he didn't understand her job. Did she have to go off so often and then there was the photo in the paper. Was she telling him the truth about her husband?

This bothered him all evening and he found sleeping difficult too. Everything was spinning round his head. The Sail

Loft, George and Jenny, Joanna and of course his aunt Jessie, what would she say or do? She might disagree altogether and want the cottage sold. In which case his plan for the Sail Loft would be a non-starter.

He got up the next morning and grabbed a very quick breakfast whilst sorting out his orders. The local shops that he already supplied came first, then the new orders and then of course something for Jenny's café. This he pondered over for some time. What would be a suitable design? He thought of a surfer, but perhaps that was rather insensitive considering her back injury. Archaeology was next. Something using the Celtic motif perhaps. Then it came to him. He knew just what to make and he would start now before he did anything else.

Apart from a short break for lunch, Ben spent the whole day working on Jenny's piece. By the end of the afternoon he had finished and placed it in his drying cabinet.

The phone rang. He picked it up. "Hello."

"Hello Ben, its Jessie here. How are you?"

"I'm fine. Isn't it about time you came back? I need to discuss things with you."

"I am coming back. That's why I've phoned. I needed to be here longer than I thought, but I've sorted everything out now. How's the sale going?"

"That's what I want to talk to you about. It's to do with Uncle Tom's things in the Sail Loft."

"Oh, that's mostly rubbish, just his bits and pieces. I never used to go in there. I should throw it all out if I were you."

"It's not that easy Jessie. I can't go into it over the phone. When exactly are you coming back?"

"On Friday. I'm arriving at Penzance station at four thirty. Can you meet me?"

"Yes, of course I can. Do I need the car or can we manage on the bus?"

"Oh, the bus will do. I haven't got that much with me. I'll

see you on Friday then Ben."

"Yes, all right, I'll see you then. Bye."

Now she was coming back Ben knew he would have to make a real decision about the Sail Loft. Not give his Aunt lots of alternatives. Like Jenny said, go for one and stick to it. Be positive, not his usual indecisive self.

He washed and changed and made sure he'd got the clay out of his fingernails. Ben picked up the phone again and dialled.

"Harbour café and restaurant, how can I help you?"

"Hi Jenny, its Ben."

"Oh hi, what's up?"

"Nothing. Are you very busy tonight?"

"We're quite well booked up, why?"

"I was wondering if you could find me a space. I thought I'd like to sample your evening menu for a change."

"Of course we can. I've got a table free at eight thirty. Will that do?"

"Yes, that's great. Oh and would you have time to talk to me while I'm there?"

"I might if I can find a few minutes."

"Good, I'll see you later then."

"Yes, all right. And you will remember we don't serve raspberry jam in the evenings!"

"Yes, of course. See you. Bye."

"Bye Ben."

Jenny put down the phone slowly wondering what Ben wanted to see her about. She worried about him sometimes particularly as he lived on his own and didn't seem to have many friends. Except this estate agent he'd met who was always going away. Very odd she thought.

Ben, on the other hand, had no such worries. He was thinking only of his ideas for the Sail Loft and trying to get everyone's agreement. His Aunt was coming back on Friday and he wanted to enlist Jenny's support. If anyone could persuade Aunt Jessie then she could. After all Jessie had asked her to keep an eye on things whilst she was away.

He had to let Jenny know what his idea was too and make sure she and George helped him sort out Uncle Tom's hoard in the Sail Loft.

His next problem was what to wear, but then it was only Jenny's place and she wouldn't mind what he went in. He hadn't much choice anyway so he put on a clean shirt, his jeans and a jacket.

As he walked round the harbour to Jenny's he looked up at the welcoming lights flickering in the windows. She had certainly made her restaurant look inviting at night. As he opened the door, the smell of food, cigarettes and warm air hit him.

"Ah there you are Ben. Come on in. I've put you on this table nearer the kitchen. More chance to talk. Is that all right?"

"It's fine Jenny, thank you."

Ben ran his eyes over the menu, but didn't really take it all in. He wasn't used to eating out on his own and felt very conspicuous. He needn't have worried. No-one was paying him any attention at all.

"Right Ben, what would you like?"

"Melon to start with please."

"Don't laugh, but we put a sauce on it, with raspberries in."

"Great! After that I'm not sure. What do you recommend?"

"You could try the mackerel."

"No, I don't think so, not after that boat trip."

"All right then, how about a peppered steak with mushrooms, fried peppers and aubergines."

"Can I have chips with it?"

"Of course you can. How do you like your steak?"

"Medium rare."

Jenny disappeared with his order and reappeared with a

bottle of red wine and two glasses. She sat next to him and poured out the wine handing one to Ben.

"Right, cheers. Now what is it that you need to talk to me about so urgently?"

Ben was somewhat taken aback by her directness and as usual stumbled over his words.

"Really, what I want to do Jenny is to enlist your support for what I want to do with the Sail Loft."

"George and I said we'd help you sort it out. Is that all?"

Claire, Jenny's waitress, brought his melon.

"Thanks Claire."

"There you are Ben, raspberries!"

"Now listen Jenny, Aunt Jessie is coming back on Friday and I've to tell her that I'm planning to develop the Sail Loft and her cottage. To do that I need you to back me up. She trusts you, she values your opinion. Will you help me please?"

"I'll consider it Ben."

Then she smiled and continued.

"Of course I'll help you. You'll need someone with some business experience behind you. Mind you, if you're going to have a café in there too, I want to run it."

"You couldn't do that. You've already got this one."

"Oh, I know, but I'm not letting another one start up without having a share in it!"

With that Jenny left him to his meal and left Claire serving.

Ben watched her again, like he had when he was in the garden having his cream tea. Her auburn hair was tied up and she was wearing a well cut dress, pale blue with a subtly coloured flower design. She looked every part the owner and seemed to know most of the people there. A far cry from their holiday days sitting on the harbour wall. She had achieved so much in a way, he was really proud of her.

Jenny turned and caught him staring at her. She smiled, winked at him and disappeared into the kitchen. Ben got on with his food, but every now and then sneaked a look at Jenny as if making sure she was all right.

Ben enjoyed his meal and had a quick word with Jenny before leaving. The restaurant had filled up while he was there and she was now very busy. He stood outside for a while looking out to sea and then up at the sky. He watched the stars and then remembered what Joanna had said.

The breeze off the sea was cool and Ben walked slowly past his Aunt Jessie's house. He stood and looked at it and imagined what he could turn it into, but all he could see was his reflection in the window.

As Friday drew nearer Ben enlisted George's help too, in his plan for the Sail Loft. He had to make sure he could present a water tight case to his Aunt Jessie, so that she saw he meant business. Jenny would help with finances and George with the possible sale potential of the books and antiques. All he needed now was to contact Joanna, easier said than done, to get a firm, up to date assessment of the cottage's value.

"Hello, is Joanna Trewick back in the office, please?"

"Just a moment…hello yes?"

"Is that you Joanna, its Ben."

"Oh hi, I've just got back, how are you?"

"I'm fine. Look, how busy are you? I need to discuss something with you."

"Hang on. I'll check what's in the diary for today. This afternoon about three. I could manage that."

"That'll be fine. I'll meet you in the car park down by the harbour."

"All right, I'll see you at three, bye."

Very business like Ben thought. Not even a hint of anything else. No mention of her flat or stars close together in the night sky.

He put these thoughts out of his mind in order to concentrate on firing his newly made pots. It was the first time he'd had so many orders and knew if he didn't keep working he'd never get them finished. The piece he'd made for Jenny was already fired, but waiting to be glazed. He had to keep it well hidden just in case she or anyone else saw it before it was ready.

There were two craft shops that sold his work, one in the village and one in Penzance. He always delivered the orders himself. The one in the village was easy as it wasn't far from his cottage, but the one in Penzance caused him problems. He couldn't get near it by car as it was in a pedestrian precinct so he went by bus. The main problem was that he could only carry so much at a time and it usually took him two trips.

So as Joanna was coming later he decided to just deliver to the shop in the village. This he duly did and was pleased to find that most of the last order had been sold. Also, he came away with another order. Things were looking up.

Ben went down to the car park early and sat on a bench near the harbour wall reading his paper. The sun was out, there were people on the beach and a few children swimming in the harbour. He always wondered why people swam in the harbour as the water always looked dirty.

He looked up and across the harbour at the boats and the visitors drinking at "The Ship". The bus had just arrived so even more people spilt into the village. His eyes came round the car park. No sign of Joanna. He returned to reading his newspaper.

After a while he looked at his watch. It was three fifteen. Where was she, or was she going to vanish to another part of the country again? He folded up his paper and walked slowly towards the car park. He watched every car going in and every car going out. Still no sign of Joanna. He did this for a while before looking at his watch again. Three thirty. Where was she?

At quarter to four he gave up and walked home feeling pretty let down. Back home he went straight out into the garden and checked his kiln. It was fine. He picked two dead heads off his rose bush and went inside the cottage.

Ben sat at the kitchen table making a list of what he was going to tell his Aunt. He wrote in detail and in order, so that he could get his thoughts straight. He couldn't settle to this, so he went out into the garden again and just wandered around. He even checked the kiln again too. He tried making some more pots, but the clay didn't seem to want to work in his hands. He stood in the corner of the garden that overlooked the village. He followed the line of the roof tops right round to the far end of the harbour. He could see Jenny's café. It seemed to be bursting with people. The sun had brought them out today. Some were even leaning against the outside eating ice-cream. He didn't feel in the mood to join them. At this moment he needed to be on his own, safe in his own thoughts.

The phone rang. He could only just hear it from the end of the garden.

"Hello, Ben Treloar."

"Hi, it's Joanna. I'm sorry Ben, I've had to come back up to Exeter. I won't be back until the middle of next week. What did you need to talk to me about?"

"You might have let me know you weren't coming, I've wasted the whole afternoon now. I needed to talk to you abut my Aunt's cottage. She's coming back on Friday."

"I'm sorry Ben. Things just happened. You know what it's like. If it's really urgent talk to one of my colleagues. All they need to do is look at my notes."

"All right I might do that. I'll see you sometime. Bye."

"Bye Ben. I hope your Aunt likes your plans."

With that Joanna was cut off. Ben had heard enough, he'd returned the receiver to its resting place.

What was she playing at? He was now annoyed and irritated. She never told him anything until the last minute or until it was too late for him to do anything about it. He needed a drink.

First he went to the end of the garden and looked down at the harbour. George's boat was tied up. He must be in his shop. He'd go and see if he'd like a drink too. Ben locked up and went down to George's bookshop.

"George, anyone in your shop at the moment?" Ben shouted as he stuck his head round the door.

"No, not that I can see. Why? What's the rush?"

"Come for a drink George. Lock up and come to the Ship."

Hang on a minute. I'll have to check the sales against the money first. Shut the door for me and put the closed sign up."

Ben did that and then fidgeted about looking at the books while George hurriedly sorted out his money and receipts.

"You didn't tell me you'd got a decent book on pottery glazes in here, George."

"Oh, have I? Probably came in when I was out on the boat and Barbara put it there."

"I haven't seen Barbara for a while. Is she all right?"

"Oh yes, she's staying with our daughter in London for a few days. That's why I'm more tied to the shop than usual."

"Right I'll have this book then George, here you are. I've only got a twenty pound note."

"That's all right, I've got a fiver in my pocket. Here you are."

"You can't keep letting me have discount George, you'll go out of business."

"Don't be daft. You're a friend I like to help out. After all, I know you'll make good use of the book. So I'm helping an up and coming potter. Come on Ben, let's go. I've finished here."

They walked to the pub chatting about glazes and Ben's new ideas for designs. They sat at a table in the window next to the fire. Ben with red wine and George with his usual pint.

"Now Ben, tell me what all the fuss is about. I've never known you drink so much."

"I needed a drink tonight George. You know I've been seeing Joanna Trewick from the Estate Agents."

"Not very often though from what you've been saying."

"I know. Well, she was supposed to be here this afternoon. I wanted to talk to her about the sale of Aunt Jessie's house. She phoned after I'd hung around for ages to say she was in Exeter again."

"So you're none too pleased?"

"That's putting it mildly. It's not just this business with the house and Sail Loft, it's our relationship too. It's important to me."

"Is it important to her as well though Ben? If she keeps going off as you say, she can't think much of you can she? Perhaps you're useful in that you're here when she needs to have some company."

"I don't honestly know George. When I saw her the other night I thought she really felt something for me."

"Did she say so though?"

"No she didn't, but I'm in love with her George. So what's she messing about at?"

"You've told her you love her have you?"

"Yes, and she has never said it back to me."

"Well maybe she doesn't feel the same as you and is just out for a good time."

"Do you think so? I'm so confused George and it's not as if I haven't been through this before."

"Well, I didn't like to say anything, but it was something like this that brought you down here in the first place."

"You'd have thought I'd have learned from that wouldn't you. When you're in love though, rational thought takes a back seat."

"Well you could say that, but with your experience, surely

you ought to be able to stand back and take a more logical view of matters. Look at the situation you're in from 'outside' like I do or Jenny does."

"That's easy for you to say, as after all, you are outside looking in. I'm caught up in the middle of it all. I'm in the centre of the maze and there's no way out. You and Jenny are standing on the observation platform watching me going round in circles and always coming back to the same place."

"Ah yes, but you could be up there with us."

"How, I don't see that."

"It's easy really Ben. We're here now talking about how you feel and that you can't see an escape route from where you are."

"Yes, I'm with you so far."

"Right, firstly your aunt Jessie isn't here, so you can make a decision about her cottage and the Sail Loft. Get it straight in your mind. Be definite about what you want. Secondly, Joanna Trewick. Her involvement simply is that she provided you with a valuation on the cottage. Ignore any feelings you have for her. You don't need her there when you talk to Jessie. You have the valuation and could in fact talk to a colleague of hers, or another estate agent. Thirdly, there's your business. You're a potter, that's what you came here to do. It's taking off, so that's your personal motivation. Make a success of it. You're nearly there. Fourth and finally, you've included Jenny and me in all this. We live here, we know you, and we know Jessie and we'll both support you. Stand back Ben, while we're here having a drink and put your mind to it. It'll become clear and you'll know what to do. I had to do it when I retired, Jenny had to do it after her accident and your Aunt Jessie is in the middle of doing it now. That leaves you. Only you can make the move and see clearly where you want to be. You've done it before, do it again, but this time decide now not in a year or two's time. Don't let the chance slip away."

Ben had sat completely still through all of this taking it in. He always knew George was good with people and knowing how they thought and acted, but he didn't realise he knew him as well as he did. He took a sip of his wine whilst he thought about what George had said. He was right about Joanna's involvement not being vital, but she was important to him. Well, he thought she was, even if nobody else did. He enjoyed her company and knew he loved her. He was sure of that, whatever she was doing. It was only her job taking her away. No-one else.

He could also see how easy it was for George and Jenny to see what was going on. They were only involved if he let them be or they wanted to be. Aunt Jessie needed to be persuaded. Well he thought she did. What had Jenny already told her? Had she explained to Jessie what was being planned? Jessie had asked Jenny to keep an eye on things. How close an eye, he wondered.

"George, let me ask you this. I've been making all these plans and telling you and Jenny about them."

"Yes, you have."

"Well, can I trust Jenny? You know Jessie asked her to keep an eye on things for her."

"Yes I do and I can assure you she's done just that, no more. Surely after all these years you know Jenny well enough to know that she wouldn't let either you or your Aunt Jessie down, don't you?"

"I do really. I suppose that after what happened to me, before I came down here and with what's going on with Joanna, I find it hard to trust anyone anymore."

"You don't trust me then, Ben?"

"Of course I do otherwise I wouldn't have told you all this and how I feel."

"So who is it you don't trust?"

"Women, I suppose."

"What all of them, or just those you come in contact with?"

"No, well I've had some bad relationships. You know, they've not worked out."

"So you mean women."

"Yes I do."

"So you'd trust Jenny then?"

"I'm not sure."

"You haven't had a relationship with her that's gone wrong have you?"

"No I haven't. I've known her a long time as a friend."

"You trusted her when you were children and you trusted her enough recently to tell her what you were planning."

"Yes I did."

"You're also very proud of her success aren't you and the way she handled her back injury."

"Yes I am. All right George, I get the point. Jenny is trustworthy and I shouldn't doubt her."

"Quite. Spot on Ben. Now go and get another drink and we'll decide what to do next."

When Ben had got the drinks, he and George talked at length about how they would, or rather how Ben would, approach his Aunt Jessie with his plan. They decided Ben would have to be completely honest and open about what he wanted to do and hope that Aunt Jessie understood and agreed.

"Right, now we've decided that, we need to speak to someone else about it don't we Ben?"

"Do we George?"

"Yes Ben, there are two of us supporting you, not just me."

"Oh, you mean Jenny. She'll agree wont she?"

"Don't assume anything Ben. If we go ahead without talking to her she may be upset and you may lose a valuable ally."

"So what do you suggest George?"

"Presumably she's working this evening."

"Isn't she always? Never stops does she."

"Right, drink up Ben. Let's go and see her now."

With that they finished their drinks, said goodbye to Jack and left the pub. It was cooler now, but still a clear evening with visitors milling about eating ice-cream or chips from the shop round the corner.

They walked up the slope to the café. Jenny was sitting outside on a stool staring out to sea and didn't see them.

"Hi Jenny."

"Hello you two. I didn't see you coming. I was just thinking what a great evening it would be for catching the surf. The tide's just right."

"You still think about surfing then?"

"Yeah once it's in your blood, you know when the best waves will be out there. That stays with you whether you can surf or not. It's all right Ben don't look so worried. It doesn't bother me anymore, but I can still dream cant I?"

"Of course you can. Have you got a minute to talk to us Jenny?"

"Do I look busy?"

"No, you don't. That's unusual."

"I always have a break now, it's just that you're not very often around to see me."

"Well, we've been down 'The Ship' having a drink and talking about Aunt Jessie coming back on Friday. So we'd like to put our thoughts to you in the hope you'll agree."

"What if I don't? I might feel put out that you talked to George first and not to me or that you didn't talk to us both together."

"I know that was the idea, but things got rather out of hand today and I needed to talk to someone and George was there."

"It's all right Ben, I don't mind at all. I've been so busy

today I wouldn't have been able to talk to you anyway."

"So you'll be there on Friday then, when I talk to Jessie?"

"What time is she going to be here?"

"I'm meeting her off the 4.30pm train. So by the time we're here and organised, about this time I suppose."

"That's ideal, as you can see it's when I have my break. So what are you going to tell Jessie?"

Ben outlined what he hoped to say and that if George and Jenny could back him up that would be great."

"Look Ben, I know you haven't been through everything in the Sail Loft yet, but I think I may be able to help."

"How's that George?"

"If I go through all the books with you we can get an estimate of how much they're worth. Then we can add that to the possible price of the motorbike. If we do that with everything you'll have a much better idea of what everything is worth."

"I could help with the catering side of things if you're really determined to have a small café and let out part of the cottage."

"Thank you both, that will be helpful and just what I need."

"Have you had an update on the valuation since you spoke to Joanna Trewick Ben?" Jenny asked.

"No I haven't."

"Gone away again has she?"

"Yes she has and George and I decided we didn't need her advice at the moment. We'd stick with the original valuation."

"Right, so Jenny and I will meet you down at your Aunt's on Friday and hope that she's agreeable to our plan."

"Yes George, that's fine."

"Well I must get home or Barbara will be phoning from London wondering where I am. See you Friday, if not before."

George left the two of them sitting outside the restaurant watching the sky grow darker.

"Stars are bright tonight Ben."

"Yes they are. There's one for everyone you know."

He said this without thinking.

"What?"

"Oh never mind. Just something I heard once."

"You do come out with some strange things these days Ben. I don't know that these 'new friends' of yours are doing you much good."

She turned towards Ben as she said it and smiled.

"You like winding me up, don't you Jenny, you didn't used to do this at all."

"Well you didn't used to make such a fool of yourself."

"What do you mean?"

"I know its none of my business, but I think I've known you long enough to be completely open with you, haven't I?"

"Yes. Go on. Get it off your chest."

"It's just that since you've come down here you've made friends in the village who don't want to see you get hurt. I don't just mean me and George, but people like Jack in the pub who knew your uncle and aunt and remember you here, as a boy, like I do."

"So you're telling me I shouldn't have anything to do with Joanna are you?"

"In a way Ben, but I'm not trying to interfere, I don't know her. You do, but it does seem strange to me that she keeps going away so much."

"She's an estate agent. Sometimes they have to deal with properties outside their area. She's very high up in the business."

"You don't have to justify her to me Ben. Remember I've known you a long time and I know you've been hurt before. I care about you and I don't want to see you upset like you obviously were today. It'll only affect your work. You're getting the recognition you deserve, so stick with that and don't go headlong into another relationship without thinking things through carefully first."

Jenny looked him straight in the eye, smiled, kissed him on the cheek and went inside the restaurant.

"End of lecture Ben!" she shouted as she pushed the door shut behind her. He sat for a while thinking over what she had said. He had been too taken aback by her frankness to come up with an immediate answer. He needed to have a long hard think about what she was saying and how it might affect things with his plan for the Sail Loft.

He sat for a little longer in the hope that Jenny might come out again. She didn't. He certainly wasn't going in so he walked through the car park, past Jessie's cottage and up the hill to his own home.

Ben sat in the garden for quite a while, sipping a glass of red wine. He'd now taken to buying bottles for home consumption, rather than the odd glass in the pub. He thought he'd better have some in the house for visitors. Whilst sitting there he noticed the kiln had stopped firing, but he was too lazy to get up and check if it had fired properly. He'd do that in the morning.

Friday came all too soon. George was a great help with the books. He sat all morning going through those that Ben had already unpacked. They also had time to look briefly through the other rooms in the Sail Loft to estimate how many more there were. It was a difficult task as there was so much other stuff lying on top of the boxes.

"Do you know Ben, I think you've enough here to open a shop let alone a pottery. We're not going to be able to sort this out today you know."

"Oh, I'd hoped we could give Jessie an answer when she arrived."

"I don't think so. Let's be realistic. You've only emptied a few boxes and they're from one room. Think what else could be in the other rooms. That's why your friend Joanna put the price so high."

"So what am I going to do now George?"

"Well, your aunt's not going anywhere in a hurry is she? So why not explain that you need more time and maybe she can help."

"Yes, but all along she's not wanted anything to do with it. She told me to sort it all out. I never have understood why."

"Have you asked her?"

"No I haven't. I just presumed she didn't want to know about it because it had been Uncle Tom's."

"I think that's something you need to ask Jessie when she gets here. Then at least you'll know won't you."

"I think we've done all we can here George. Thank you for all your help."

"That's all right. I do seriously think you ought to consider having a second hand business here too, as well as your pottery."

"That'll cut across your business."

"Not really. You see, once you've sold all Tom's things, you'll still have the pottery. One takes over from the other. Think about it, along with all your other ideas. I'll see you later when Jessie's here."

"Thanks George, bye."

Ben felt as if there were obstacles at every twist and turn. What he'd thought would be a nice, simple clearing out exercise, had almost turned into a monster. Still, George's idea was a good one and a way of financing his pottery. If Aunt Jessie agreed, then all would be well, but would she?"

Ben went over everything as he waited for the bus. He'd passed George on the way, going home for lunch rather late, and he was now looking over at the harbour café wondering what Jenny would say to Jessie, or had she already been in contact? After all, she was supposed to be keeping an eye on things for her. Then he thought about how outspoken Jenny could be, how she'd left when they last spoke. She had actually kissed him on the cheek, after all she'd said. She'd never done that before.

The bus arrived and Ben waited patiently for everyone to get off. They were mostly holiday makers or he thought they must be as he didn't recognise anyone. He paid and sat at the back, something he didn't usually do!

"Hi Ben, how are you?"

It was Claire, Jenny's waitress. She came and sat in front of him.

"I'm fine. Not working today?"

"No, I mostly work in the evenings. I'm usually at college during the day. Are you going to meet your Aunt?"

"Does everyone in the village know what I'm doing?"

"I shouldn't think so, but Jenny does, which is why I've got to be back to cover for her tonight in case she's held up."

"I see. How is Jenny today?"

"Fine, why?"

"Oh, no reason."

"She was cross with you the other night wasn't she?"

"No she wasn't."

He wished she'd go away. He didn't want to talk, he wanted to think.

"Well she came charging back into the restaurant and got really ratty with us. You were still sitting outside. I told her to come out and talk to you but she wouldn't."

"Thank you Claire. I needed to know that right now."

Ben tried to sound disinterested and stared out of the window. Claire carried on.

"Oh, I'm sorry. I didn't mean to upset you. She likes you a lot you know, but I don't think she can tell you herself, too shy. Do you know what I mean?"

"Yes Claire."

"Well I said to her, you go out there and tell him but she wouldn't. She told me to mind my own business. I was only trying to help."

"Yes Claire, I'm sure you were."

"Oh, this is my stop. I'm going to see my mum. Bye Ben, it's been really nice talking to you."

"Bye Claire."

Ben sat back in his seat and sighed. Thank goodness she'd got off. At least he'd have a little time left to get his head straight before meeting Aunt Jessie.

Penzance being a terminus made it easy to see when the train arrived, so Ben stood behind the railings staring along the track. Nothing. He looked at his watch. Four thirty five. It's late. Then an announcement to the effect that the train had been delayed at Plymouth and would be arriving in approximately ten minutes.

Ben found a bench and sat watching everyone wandering aimlessly about, some agitated, looking at their watches, others happily talking to each other and the rest, like him, bored.

The train arrived and people emerged from its carriages. He tried to make out Aunt Jessie, but there were too many faces. So he stood and waited, she'd probably find him before he noticed her. Still people trooped off the platform, but no sign of Aunt Jessie. Then in the distance ambling along, completely unaware of anyone else, was Jessie. She seemed smaller than usual, older, but still clutching her one suitcase that she took everywhere. Her small round glasses were perched, as always, on the end of her nose.

"Hello Ben, there you are. How nice to be back."

"I thought for one moment you weren't on the train at all."

"I was right at the back, almost in the last seat. Short walk at the start of the journey, long one at the end!"

"Quite. Now let me take your case. There's a bus in five minutes."

As they walked to the bus stop Jessie rambled on about the journey, how long it had taken and how a nice man sitting opposite her had gone to get her some coffee. They talked briefly about her relatives while they waited for the bus. Nothing startling. Everyone was well, sent their regards to Ben and wished she wasn't leaving.

The bus ride back was uneventful. Fortunately Claire did not get on, so they continued talking about her visit to the relatives. She hardly ever referred to them by name, always as 'the relatives'. Ben was never quite sure how many of them there were and he only knew one or two by name, Jessie had always been the independent one in the family and in some way had been rather cut off from the rest. Apparently, they hadn't approved of her marriage to Tom and said it would never last, but it had. Now she was emigrating they seemed to be more friendly again and were trying to persuade her to stay in this country.

Ben just hoped she would be sympathetic to his ideas. Having George and Jenny there would help he was sure. They arrived at her cottage and Ben opened the door.

"It's good to be back Ben. It just looks the same, except for these piles of books and whatever that is stacked up in the yard."

"I've been sorting Tom's things out in the Sail Loft. It's taking longer than I expected."

"Let's have a nice cup of tea and you can tell me all about it."

"No, I'll get it, you sit down. I've quite a few things I want to talk to you about Aunt Jessie, so make yourself comfortable."

"Oh dear, that sounds ominous."

"No, don't worry. I think they're good positive things."

There was a knock at the door. It was Jenny and George. They'd arrived together so at least Ben could involve everyone at once.

"Hello Jessie, how are you?" they both said together. "It's good to see you back here again."

"What is this, are you all ganging up on me or is this just a welcoming party. I've not been away for that long you know. Well, not as long as I'm planning to be away in the future!"

"Ben's done a lot of thinking while you've been away and we are both involved. So we thought that it was only fair that we were here too," explained George.

"What about you Jenny, you're quiet, aren't you going to say something?"

"No I'm not Jessie because you know full well what I think already. I think you need to be completely honest with Ben too."

"What is all this Aunt Jessie? I don't understand. What has Jenny been telling you?"

"It's not what you think Ben. As you know I asked Jenny to keep an eye on things here for me!"

"Yes I do. I couldn't be here all the time."

"I know that and that is why Jenny has been really good in doing what I asked."

"So Jenny's been spying on me and all the planning I've been doing, has that been passed back to you too?"

"No, not exactly. Now listen Ben, Jenny is very loyal to me and she's been very loyal to you too."

"It doesn't sound like it."

"Let me finish. I knew that once you started sorting things out for me here and found Tom's things you'd start having grand ideas about the cottage, the Sail Loft and all his things. So I asked Jenny to see that you kept your feet on the ground, but from what she's told me, you've done that yourself. So I do know what you've decided to do and I agree. Tom wanted you to have all his things, that's your inheritance. Do what you want with it all. I'll sell you the house for a nominal fee. After all, I don't need the money. Tom left me very well off."

Ben didn't know what to say. There was so much for him to take in. All along, Jenny in particular and George to a lesser extent had known what was going on. In a way he was relieved that he didn't have to twist his Aunt's arm to get his way, but in another he felt foolish and a little let down by his friends. However, he couldn't bring himself to say so, as both Jenny and George had, nonetheless, been very supportive.

"Well Ben, that was a long silence. What are you thinking?" Asked Jessie.

"I'm really delighted Aunt Jessie. Thank you so very much or should I say thank you and Uncle Tom."

"You should indeed."

"Just one more thing though. What exactly is this nominal fee? How much are we talking about?"

"Oh I should think the price of a motorbike should do it. Don't you, George?"

"Oh yes indeed, I think that's spot on."

Ben couldn't believe what he was hearing. The price of a motorbike. He'd only got bits of one and had no idea how much it was worth.

"The price of a motorbike, Aunt Jessie, might vary a great deal. As you probably already know, I've only found a few parts so far."

"I know that, remember I have a good informant in Jenny! There is however one place I don't think you've looked yet."

"I've searched the Sail Loft. The large pieces wouldn't fit into the boxes.."

"I know that too. Now, have you had a good look in the garage?"

"What garage? These cottages don't have garages do they?"

"No, not built on, but we owned two. They're up the hill behind the old chapel. There's a chain padlocked across the drive in front. We haven't used them for years. Now, George, you stay and have tea with me. Jenny, take Ben up to the garages. You've got a key I think."

"Yes I have. Come on, Ben. I'll show you where they are."

Ben didn't look too pleased at the prospect of being with

Jenny, but he went to please his Aunt. He didn't want to upset her on her first day back.

Ben followed Jenny out of the cottage and up the hill. They didn't speak. Ben followed slightly behind Jenny, noticing her auburn hair and how it shone in the light. They walked past the chapel and there tucked in behind were the two garages. Ben was surprised. He hadn't noticed them before, but then if you weren't looking for them you wouldn't see them where they were.

"Here we are Ben. Do you want to open them?"

Jenny handed him the key. Ben took the key without saying a word.

"Hang on a minute Ben. You're not going to ignore me forever are you? I haven't done anything underhand Ben. You know Jessie had asked me to keep an eye on things and that's what I did. Yes, I knew she wanted you to have her cottage, but both she and Tom talked about it for years. I was sworn to secrecy and only told because I'd known you so long. They wanted you to find your own feet down here first. That's just what you've done, so now Jessie's told you. Come on, we've all got your best interests at heart. Now open that door."

"Jenny, I'm sorry. I didn't realise…"

"I know Ben, open the door!"

With that Ben opened the first garage door. They pulled the double doors open together and stood back in amazement.

"I don't believe this. Is it really what I think it is?"

There standing before them was a gleaming 'E' type Jaguar sports car. Bright red with a very old original number plate. Three letters and three numbers.

They walked around it not daring to touch it. Jenny looked across at Ben and smiled. He returned the smile.

"This is fabulous. Did you know about this Jenny?"

"No, not what was in here. I knew about the garages, not what was in them. We'd better look in the other one quickly."

They closed the doors on the Jaguar and locked them again. Ben handed the key to Jenny and told her to open the second set of doors. Inside, they found two complete motorbikes covered by dust sheets and the missing parts that fitted with what Ben had found in the Sail Loft.

"This is amazing Jenny. I can't take it all in. These bikes and the car together must be worth a fortune. I can't possibly accept all this from Jessie."

"Ben, she and Tom wanted you to have this. They thought about it long and hard. You're the son they never had. They used to love it when you came to stay. You were always so interested in them and their life together. They never forgot that and this is how they wanted to repay you."

"Jessie's daughter in America should have all this, surely?"

"Ben, their daughter left years ago and made a new life over there. She's done very well and is now trying to repay Jessie for all the years she's been away. It's now the time for them to be together. She knows all about this too you know. Tom left a lot to her in his will too, not that she needed it!"

"I see, so I can really get on and do what I'd planned then?"

"Yes Ben. Just do it for once, stop dithering. Grasp the opportunity and go for it."

"Right Jenny, I will. You and George, you will still help won't you?"

"Of course we will. Come on, lock up and lets get back to Jessie and George, they'll be wondering what's happened to us."

They walked back down the hill to Jessie's cottage, talking about what they had found in the garages and wondering if Jessie really knew the true value of the car and the bikes. Jenny thought she probably had a fair idea of their worth.

"Well." Said Jessie as they entered the cottage, "What did you find?"

"An E-type Jag, two motorbikes and the missing parts from

the one in the Sail Loft. Do you really know what they're worth Aunt Jessie?"

"Yes I do Ben. I had the E-type valued last year and Jack in the pub knows the value of the bikes."

"Does he now," replied Ben,. "Well he did a pretty good bit of play acting when I told him about what I'd found. You wait till I see him."

"You'll be saying it's a conspiracy again in a minute Ben. So before you do, it isn't. It's what I told you before, lots of people taking an interest in you" explained Jenny.

"All right, I believe you. Now Aunt Jessie, we must get you settled back in here."

"Not just yet you won't Ben. I've booked a table at Jenny's place and if we don't get a move on we'll be late, won't we Jenny?"

"You will indeed. Right George, you come with me and let Ben bring Jessie in about ten minutes."

Jenny and George left together with George muttering something that Ben couldn't quite catch but it sounded like Barbara at the end. So he presumed George was going home to his wife and not eating with them.

"Well Ben, are you convinced now about my intentions for you?"

"Yes I am Jessie, and thank you very much. I'll try and make a real go of this."

"Jenny's been telling me about the success you had in Exeter with the exhibition. It really went very well I gather."

"Yes it did, and I've got months of work out of it."

"So there you are, you're a success. The move down here does seem to have worked for you at last."

"Yes it has, and I'd like to make a success of my plans for the Sail Loft too. I really do appreciate what you've done for me. I can't thank you enough Jessie."

"You know it wasn't just me Ben. Tom wanted to help you

and we agreed we'd do all we could for you but that you had to make the first moves yourself. We weren't going to make it easy for you."

"No, I can see that now and how everyone has been so supportive. Thank you."

They locked up the cottage and walked slowly round the harbour as the early evening light sent strange shadows across the water.

"Ben, before we get to the restaurant, can I ask you something personal?"

"Yes of course. What is it?"

"Well, I was wondering if you've met anyone you like down here?"

"Yes I have Jessie."

"Am I allowed to know who it is?"

"Her name's Joanna. She's the estate agent who valued your cottage."

"Oh."

"What's up?"

"Nothing, I just thought that you and…"

"Jenny?"

"Yes."

"Jessie, I've known her as a friend for years. You know that. We spent summers here as children, playing and sharing our ideas. She's done really well since her accident, but we're just friends, that's all."

"This Joanna. Do you see a lot of her?"

"No not really. She's away a lot working."

"I see, not really a permanent relationship then?"

"No I suppose it isn't,"

They left it there and stood leaning on the railings above the water's edge. It was another beautiful evening and Ben could see that Jessie was taking it all in.

"You'll miss this view when you're in America."

"I know but I'll keep it in my memory. At my age I have many good memories that will come back from time to time as I need them. But I'm sure there'll be many memories to cherish in the future."

With that they linked arms and sauntered up to Jenny's.

"At last, I thought you two had got lost, where have you been?"

"Just taking in the evening air and looking at the view. Ben and I decided we'd chat on the way and then thought it was a nice evening to stand and watch the world go by."

"Well now you're here. I've put you by the window, so you can spend the whole evening staring at the view!"

"Thank you Jenny. Where's George?"

"Barbara had cooked him a meal already, so he thought he'd better go and eat it."

Jenny left Ben and Jessie together for a while and let Claire take their order. Ben was relieved that Claire didn't mention having seen him on the bus. They talked through most of the meal. About Ben's plans yet again, his childhood holidays spent in the village and a lot about Tom and Jessie. Ben tried to keep off the subject of Jenny or any other friends he may have in the village.

Fortunately Jessie didn't bring up the subject either. Jenny came to see how they were getting on from time to time, but was more involved with the other guests.

After the meal Ben walked Jessie home and made sure she had all she needed before leaving. Instead of going straight home, Ben went down to the harbour and sat on the wall, in the exact place where he and Jenny used to sit.

He thought long and hard about what Aunt Jessie had said. He was sure she'd like to have seen him in a lasting relationship before she left for America. He thought about Joanna too. He didn't really know where she was or what she was doing, but he did know that he wanted to see her again.

Hopefully sooner than later.

Then there was Jenny. How kind she'd been right from when they were children. Always someone he found easy to talk to and who was always there with the right answer.

Ben jumped down from the wall and went home. Almost immediately after he'd shut the front door the phone rang.

"Hi, it's Joanna. You're in at last. How are you? Where have you been? What are you doing tonight?"

"Which one do you want me to answer first? I'm here, just got in, been out for a meal with my Aunt, I'm tired and it's almost ten o'clock. What do you want?"

"What are you going to do now Ben?"

"I told you, I'm tired. Probably go to bed. Why?"

"I'm here Ben, back in my flat. Come over please. Go on, you can't be that tired surely. I'm only a bus ride away!"

"I know you are. Look, I've had a very busy day and...oh all right. There's a bus at ten fifteen. I'll get that one. Don't go away."

"I won't. See you soon Ben. Bye."

He put down the phone. What was he doing? On an impulse he was going to meet Joanna. He loved her, that's why he was going. Love conquers all. Well sometimes it does.

He ran to the bus stop but the bus wasn't there yet. He leant on the railings again and stared up at the stars. There's one for everyone went through his mind, but his thoughts were interrupted again by a familiar voice. It was Claire.

"Where are you going Ben?"

"Into town, why?"

"Just wondered. I'm going home. Jenny let me go early. I'd have thought you'd be round your Aunt's house."

"No Claire. I'm not. I'm going to see some friends in Penzance that's all."

"Bit late isn't it?"

"No it isn't. I often go out late."

"Do you, I've never seen you before this late."

"Sometimes I drive or get picked up or get a taxi."

What was he doing? He didn't have to justify himself to Claire. Fortunately the bus came and filled up quickly. Claire found someone she knew, so he didn't have to talk to her. He did smile at her when she got off.

When the bus reached the station Ben walked the few yards to Joanna's flat. He pressed the intercom and she let him in. As she opened the door, he caught just a glimpse of her eyes and he was drawn to her once again.

"Thanks for coming Ben. You look good, it's nice to see you again."

"It's good to be here with you. You look terrific."

"Thanks. Drink?"

"I'd love one."

"I've some wine out on the balcony. Red you like, don't you?"

"Yes I do. Thank you."

"Look up there Ben. There are our stars again."

He wasn't looking. He was watching her and her every move. The eyes, her lisp, her hair and her smile. She turned to look at him.

"You're not listening to a word I'm saying Ben Treloar, are you?"

"Yes I am but I haven't seen you for a while, so I was looking and listening at the same time."

He looked into her eyes and she into his. They moved closer together and their lips met. Ben was in heaven.

The same ritual happened as before in the morning. Ben stood waiting for his bus chewing a piece of toast. Then he thought back to the last time he'd done this. Jenny had seen him getting off the bus. He must be more discreet.

So he left the bus stop and walked up into town and found a café that was open. He had a coffee and a bacon sandwich and saw no-one he knew. By the time he was out of there all the shops were open, so he spent some time browsing.

By ten o'clock he felt it was safe to get a bus back. On the way be bought some bread and some fresh vegetables. Now he felt secure and looking like a genuine early morning shopper.

He had to wait for the bus. So that added more time. He was enjoying this. No-one got on the bus that he knew until he reached Newlyn and there was Claire. He tried to make himself look small and stared out of the window but she spotted him.

"Hi Ben, you been shopping?"

"Yes Claire."

"What you bought then, anything interesting?"

"No, only bread and vegetables."

"You could have bought them in the village."

"Yes I know, but it's fresher in town."

"Oh is it. Do you know, my mum bought a lettuce the other day and when she washed it, it was all black in the middle. We have to be careful at Jenny's place too, 'cos the people keep coming in to check on everything. She buys her vegetables from the wholesaler. He delivers. She doesn't have to go and get it."

Ben sat listening and wishing she'd go away, but said nothing in reply.

"I'm working all day today. What are you doing, more of your pots?"

"Probably. I haven't decided."

"Jenny, she does lots of writing in her spare time. Always writing she is, never stops. She says its archaeology or something. You know, what she used to do. I think she misses it, don't you?"

"Yes, I expect she does."

He didn't want to hear all this, but was interested to hear about Jenny writing. She hadn't mentioned it. Fortunately, before Claire could start up again, they reached the village and Ben got off quickly and went straight home.

There, he slumped yet again into a chair and thought back to the previous evening and night. Joanna had been all there for him, just like the last time, but something in the back of his mind bothered him. He wasn't sure what it was, only that he felt she was going to disappear yet again to another job.

The phone rang. It was Joanna.

"Just thought I'd check you were back all right. Not spotted this time."

"I stayed in town for a while. Only just got back. Thank you for last night. It was good seeing you again."

"Yes, and you came when I called you too. I thought you'd find an excuse not to come."

"You were very persuasive and I love you too."

"Yes I know. Now look Ben," she said quickly changing the subject, "What are you doing next weekend?"

"Nothing, why?"

"I've got to go to a presentation and meal in Truro on Saturday and wondered if you'd like to come as my 'partner'. It's all paid for. I'll drive you there."

"I'd love to Joanna. Thank you."

"Great, I'll pick you up about seven, is that all right?"

"Yes fine. Oh, what do I wear? Is it posh?"

"Have you got a suit?"

"Yes, somewhere, if I can still get into it. Mind you, I may have a choice!"

"Right, I'll see you Saturday, about seven, in a suit!"

"Yes, I'll look forward to it, bye."

He sat back in the chair. This sounded good. At last he felt as if she was really interested in him. Then he panicked. Where were his suits? He hadn't worn one since he'd moved here. Could he still get into them? He went up to his bedroom and rummaged about amongst the unpacked cases he'd thrown into the back of the wardrobe. He found them, rather crumpled, but they were there and still looking much the same, thank goodness. He tried them on and they fitted. In fact, if anything they were not as tight as they used to be. So maybe he'd lost weight and not even noticed.

At least he'd have the week to have the suits cleaned and make sure they were all right. In the meantime, he knew he had to make a start on the Sail Loft. It was good that his Aunt was there now, at least he could ask her about things.

Ben spent most of the week sharing his time between the Sail Loft and working on his pottery orders. Aunt Jessie usually made him lunch and she'd join him some evenings up at his cottage. They decided that on Friday they would eat at Jenny's so booked a table.

Almost all of one room had been full of boxes of books and it was sorting these out that took the most time. Jessie was good in that she'd read inscriptions inside the front cover, tell Ben who they were and let him decide whether he wanted to keep them or not. Between them, they were quite ruthless, but Ben insisted he kept all the ones Tom and Jessie had given each other.

By the time Friday arrived they had sorted the books. George was going to look too, so that he could decide on which ones he wanted for his shop. The rest Ben would sell from the Sail Loft. The next job was to tackle the remaining rooms, but they decided to put that off until the next week.

Ben and Jessie changed before going to Jenny's. They hadn't realised just how dirty they'd got sorting the books. The weather wasn't good. It was wet, dark and stormy as Ben and Jessie walked up to Jenny's, desperately holding an umbrella that the wind was trying to wrench from them.

The restaurant was about half full and Jenny welcomed them and helped them off with their wet coats.

"What a night. It's the worst it's been for weeks. How are you both? How's the Sail Loft going?"

"Really well thanks Jenny. We were more dirty than tired. It's been a great asset having Aunt Jessie here to help."

"I'm sure it has. Now over here. I've found you a nice quiet corner tonight, so you two can chatter away in peace."

"Thank you Jenny. You are thoughtful girl, isn't she Ben?"

"Yes Jessie, she always is."

"Right, decide what you both want and I'll get Claire to take you order."

Ben was dreading seeing Claire again. He only hoped she didn't go on about seeing him on the bus. She didn't. She took their order and disappeared into the kitchen.

Jenny brought their food and sat with them.

"I hear you've been early morning shopping in Penzance Ben? Our village produce not good enough for you then?"

Jenny couldn't resist a chance to wind him up.

"So Claire couldn't keep her mouth shut then. She does go on you know Jenny. How on earth do you put up with her?"

"Well here, I'm the boss and she wouldn't dare start on me. Be more firm Ben. Tell her to shut up!"

"I couldn't do that!"

"I do. It's the best way to stop her. She's a good worker and says all the right things to my customers though. So what were you doing in Penzance so early, not visiting your 'new friends' again?"

Ben wasn't going to rise to the bait, it was none of her business anyway.

"I went shopping Jenny, that's all. Now stop getting at me."

"Oh do stop it you two, you're like a couple of kids. You used to get on better when you were teenagers than you do now."

Jessie had been listening and was intrigued. She too wondered why Ben had gone into Penzance so early or had he?

She'd heard all about Joanna from Jenny, so maybe he'd been there all night. So she decided to join in the banter too.

"Has Ben told you where he's going tomorrow night Jenny?"

"No he hasn't. Where are you going Ben? To see your 'new friends'?"

"Thanks a lot Jessie. I was trying to keep this quiet."

"Now that does fascinate me Ben. Must be something very special. Where are you going?"

Ben thought Jenny was beginning to sound like Claire or had she already guessed what he was doing and who he'd be with. He didn't really want to tell Jenny anything about it, but now that Jessie had got involved he'd have to.

"Oh, all right then Jenny. I suppose you'd have found out anyway. I'm going to Truro tomorrow night with Joanna Trewick, as her partner or whatever, to a presentation meal."

"Oh I see," said Jenny rather taken aback. "Posh do is it then?"

"Yes it is. I've got to wear a suit."

"Have you got one Ben? I've never seen you wear one, or have you had to buy one?"

"As it happens Jenny, I've got three and I've had them cleaned this week. All I've got to do now is choose which one."

"Perhaps Joanna will do that for you."

"Don't be silly Jenny. She's picking me up at seven so I've got to be ready."

"Is she now. How nice. I'm sure you'll enjoy yourself. I've heard about these 'do's', all booze, food and people falling over. You'll like that."

With that Jenny went back into the kitchen. Ben watched her go and thought she sounded upset that he was going off with Joanna.

"Have I upset her Jessie?"

"No I don't think so. She's so used to winding you up that

when you retaliate, she can't take it. She'll be fine. I keep telling you Ben, she's very fond of you. She doesn't get out much, working here, she's jealous that's all."

They finished their main course and Claire brought them the menu again. They chose what they wanted, but this time Claire brought it out to them. Jenny served other tables and chatted with the customers. Ben kept sneaking looks at her. Her hair shone again in the candle light and she looked so self-assured. He was sorry he'd had a go at her, but then she was always winding him up, so there wasn't really any harm in it.

At the end of the meal, they got up to pay, but Jenny reappeared and told them to sit down again. Ben was annoyed as he wanted to go home and get things sorted out for his night out in Truro.

"I'm sorry, I shouldn't have gone off like that. It's not like me at all. I'm usually very professional when I'm working. Sorry."

"You don't need to apologise Jenny. Ben and I have had a lovely evening and the meal was wonderful. I'm so glad this venture of yours has worked out so well. You must be very pleased."

"Yes I am. Thank you. There is something else before you go. I think Claire let the cat out of the bag about my new book."

"Yes, she did. When we were on the bus coming back from Penzance. What are you writing about this time?"

"Well, I've been trying to do it on the quiet, not letting anyone know until I was sure of the content. It started as another study of the ancient sites in the area, but somehow seems to be turning into a novel! So you can see it's causing me all sorts of problems at the moment. Neither one thing nor the other."

"It sounds intriguing. You must let me read it."

"Oh no Ben, not until I've finished and it's been proof read. Then maybe you might get a sneak preview."

"I'm pleased you're still carrying on with your work. I thought you lived and breathed 'The Harbour Café' and nothing else."

"No Ben, I've loads of interests but I don't go round advertising them. Come on now, get Jessie home, she's had a busy week. I'll see you both again soon."

"Thanks Jenny."

Ben and Jessie walked back round the harbour towards Jessie's cottage. She stopped and looked back at the café. Ben noticed a different look on her face as if she was dreaming.

"What's the matter?"

"Oh, I was just thinking back to when Tom and I used to sit in the café long before you or Jenny were born. How much it's changed inside, but from here it still retains its original shape and distinctive design."

"We've all moved on Jessie, but at least you have those wonderful, happy memories of Tom."

"Yes I have, and of you and Jenny too when you were young. Now look at you both, still friends, but leading very separate lives."

"Yes things have changed for both of us, but I hope we are still friends. Even if she does keep winding me up."

"She's testing you Ben. To see how far she can push you. To try and see what you are really like."

"She knows what I'm like already."

"Oh no she doesn't. You might think because you've known her a long time she understands you. You've not seen each other for a long time. She wants to get to know you all over again."

"Does she, but I'm sure I know her."

"I don't think you do Ben. She's very complex. Dig a little deeper. I think you'll be surprised with what you find."

With that Jessie turned away from him and walked to her front door.

"Goodnight Ben. Have a really good time in Truro, but remember what I've said. Think about it."

"Good night Aunt Jessie. I will."

After she'd gone in he walked back to where they'd been standing and looked up at the café. He'd known both the café, as a meeting place when he was younger and Jenny for the same length of time. He stood for a while going over what Jessie had said, but was still certain he knew Jenny as well as he ever would. He couldn't really see what his Aunt was trying to tell him.

Saturday came soon enough. Ben spent the day sorting out his clothes and trying to imagine just what it was that he was attending with Joanna. All the time, however, the thoughts that had been put into his head by his Aunt, concerning Jenny, kept recurring.

In the end Ben chose his grey suit so that he didn't look too dark and drab. He felt it suited his new image, so he added a rather bright tie to offset it. Artistic, he thought. It would be an ice-breaker. Start of a good conversation.

Joanna arrived on the stroke of seven o'clock. He was glad he was ready on time to set a good impression.

"Hi Ben, you're ready. I am impressed."

It had worked. He was pleased.

"I love the tie. Very creative. You look great."

"Thanks. You look pretty good yourself."

Ben thought that didn't sound right so he started again.

"The dress looks great, I like the colour, dark blue suits you."

"Thanks. Come on then, let's get going. We don't want to be late."

Joanna didn't hang about. He'd never been through the village so quickly in his life before. Fortunately the road to Truro wasn't that busy and Ben had hardly noticed Penzance. He just hoped there weren't any police lurking about.

Their destination turned out to be a large hall in the centre of Truro. They were met at the entrance by two enormous bouncers who checked Joanna's invitation. Once inside Joanna was greeted by nearly everyone. Ben stayed slightly behind her, but smiled and nodded his head when introduced to a few of them.

The hall was quite striking inside. There were wooden pillars supporting what at first appeared to be a very low ceiling, but once you reached the middle, realised that it was in fact a balcony. The roof above the central area was very high but well lit. The wooden panelling was enhanced by wooden sculptures of animals and strange ancient creatures.

Joanna led Ben to a large rectangular table at the far end where a group of men were sitting. Ben was introduced to them, but found it difficult to remember their names or what Joanna said they did. Joanna sat in the middle of them leaving Ben to find his place name two seats away from her right on the end. He couldn't make out the name of the man next to him but Ben decided it looked like Tarquin, but he was probably wrong. Then he looked at the man again and decided he looked like a Tarquin, so that was what Ben thought of him as.

A gong was struck and all the guests were seated. Ben tried to estimate how many there were. Two hundred, roughly, but he couldn't be sure. He let his eyes drift round the room. People were talking, laughing, smoking and drinking. They seemed very content with each other's company. He wondered how many were like him. Outsiders, just brought along as an appendage, a convenient arm to lean on.

Joanna seemed miles away, and all through the meal Ben tried to catch her eye, but each time 'Tarquin' asked him some really stupid question. In the end Ben became so irritated by him that he invented a new persona and acted out the part.

"Jolly good food this. Been to one of these before have you? What did you say your name was? You do what?"

"My name's Clay. I'm in films."

"Really? I say, how exciting. Are you down here working?"

"Oh yes, we're here on location at the moment. Filming near Godrevy. Flying back to the studio tomorrow for retakes."

"Super. How fascinating. What's it called?"

"What, the film?"

"Yeah"

"Oh it's a mystery called 'The Missing Wheelbarrow Murders'. I'm not too keen on the title myself, but the author won't change it."

"Do I know the Author?"

"Depends if you've read any of his work."

"What else has he done?"

"Only one other film, but he's written loads of books."

"What's the film?"

"The Mysterious Moving Mountain. It was a huge hit in the States."

"Really. I don't remember it."

"No you probably wouldn't. Not his best work. Where do you work?"

"I'm in the Bodmin office. Very busy you know. Not like Joanna though. She's the real high flier. That's why she's President of the Association this year."

So that was it. Why she wanted someone there with her. Why hadn't she told him, and why was she totally ignoring him now? Perhaps it was supposed to be a surprise.

"What does she have to do as President?" Ben asked.

"Well tonight she'll make her first speech and outline how she sees the Association moving forward this year. Then someone will propose a toast to her and we'll finish the wine and all go home.

"The speech she has to make. Is it usually long?"

"Oh no. But she's meant to come up with something new and dynamic. I could never do it. I'm far too dull."

Quite! Thought Ben. He now got interested in the evening. He forgot that he was unable to communicate with Joanna and waited patiently for her speech to begin. He didn't have to wait long. At eleven o'clock precisely someone called for silence and Joanna rose from her seat. It was the first time he'd really seen her all evening. She glowed in the subdued light against the background of spotlights and rising clouds of cigarette smoke.

Far from being short, the speech seemed to drag on too long for Ben's liking. Probably because it was technical in nature and he knew little about estate agencies. Joanna quoted figures and there were polite rounds of applause. When she mentioned specific people, there were cheers or groans and one or two people clapped and cheered.

Joanna concluded with a rousing sentence about adopting new approaches to sales, which was way over his head. However, to everyone else it was obviously important as they gave Joanna a standing ovation. It was only then, as she sat down, that she turned to him for the first time, winked and smiled. That was enough to turn his stomach over and for him to be swept away. Her smile always did that to him.

"Great speech, eh?"

"Yes," Ben replied weakly. He wished he could be alone with her right now, but he knew it was impossible. Tonight two hundred other people had first call on her attention. He would have to wait until later to talk to her. On the journey home most likely. Ben was right. It was one in the morning before they left. Joanna threw him the car keys and asked if he would drive. She knew he'd not been drinking.

She said very little as they drove out of Truro, only briefly replying when Ben told her how good her speech was. Ben kept talking but soon realised that Joanna was fast asleep. On reaching Penzance he parked the car at the back of the flats. He woke Joanna and helped her out of the car and into the block of flats. Going up the stairs was difficult as Joanna was like a dead weight on Ben's arms.

She fumbled for the key and almost fell into her flat as the door opened. Ben helped her into the bedroom where she collapsed on the bed and fell asleep. Ben turned off the light, closed the front door and left.

Outside, he looked up at the sky. It was a clear night and he smiled to himself as he watched the stars. There was no-one around. It was Sunday morning and very, very quiet.

Ben walked along the sea front towards Newlyn. There was no fish market to stop at tonight, no Jenny to meet on the way. He'd have a slow, lonely walk home.

That was just how it was until he neared the village. It was almost dawn and he could see the sky lightening on the horizon. He stopped above the old lifeboat station. It was a high point and there was a bench there from which he could watch the sun rise.

Ben sat completely still with his eyes on the horizon. Out in the semi-darkness he could just make out the chugging engine of a boat returning from a night's fishing. A lonely boat, alone on a still night with bows cutting a swathe through an otherwise glassy sea.

Rather like he was alone now. Sitting, thinking his own thoughts whilst watching the sun slowly rise. There was a stillness and calm about Ben. He was content. The evening had been different and quite illuminating. He had seen Joanna in a new guise. Not quite how he had thought she was at all.

There was little movement in the air. In the bushes across the road he heard rustling and somewhere over the village the first morning gull screeched. The road was empty. No cars no buses, no vans, no lorries and no noisy people. Ben tried to anticipate which would be the first vehicle along the road. He didn't have to wait long as he heard the roar of a motorbike climbing the hill out of Newlyn. It passed him in an instant. It was quiet again.

The sun rose much quicker than he'd expected. The birds and wildlife around him became a mass of sound and almost at once vehicles of all types were thundering past. He lifted his weary body from the bench and began to walk slowly, but steadily, towards the village.

It didn't take him too long but in his tired state it seemed like hours. He reached home safely without encountering anyone he knew and fell into bed.

Ben woke with a start. It was the phone. He grabbed it still in a semi-conscious state.

"Hello?"

"Ben?"

"Yes, who is it?"

"Joanna. Are you all right? You sound terrible."

"You've woken me up. What time is it?"

"Three o'clock."

"What!"

"In the afternoon. I phoned to thank you."

"What for?"

"Getting me home safely. I don't remember much about it."

"That's all right. You were drunk. Very out of it. I left you where you fell asleep."

"I know. Look, come over. I'll cook us something. Have you eaten?"

"I'm asleep. I walked home. I'm tired. When? Tonight?"

"Whenever you like. You walked home? Whatever for? You should have taken my car."

"I wanted to. I like walking. I like the fresh air. I'll see you later."

"Soon Ben. Don't go back to sleep. See you soon."

"Yes I can hear you. See you soon. Bye."

He put the phone down, put his head back on the pillow and went to sleep.

The phone range again.

"Where are you?"

"Is that you Joanna? I must have gone back to sleep. Sorry. What time did you say it was?"

"I didn't, but it's now six o'clock. Are you coming or not?"

"Yes Joanna. I'm up. I'm on my way now."

"Right, I'll see you soon then?"

"Yes, Bye."

Ben put the phone down again, rolled out of bed and made his way to the shower after which he dressed in what he could find that was clean, shaved and raced out of the door. He ran to the bus stop and miraculously there was a bus waiting.

At a quarter to seven he was standing outside Joanna's flat, ringing the bell. She opened the door. She was wearing a t-shirt and old jeans with her hair cascading over her shoulders.

"Hi, that was quick."

"Oh, I don't mess around."

"No, you just fall asleep!"

"Right, I asked for that!"

"Come on in. I hope you didn't find last night too boring?"

"No I had a wonderful chat with the guy sitting next to me. Tarquin or something. Anyway he told me all about you and that you were the President this year and had to make a speech."

"Tarquin? I don't know him."

"He said he was in the Bodmin office."

"Oh that's Terence. Wherever did you get Tarquin from?"

"It's what I thought his card said on the table."

"You fool, you didn't call him that did you?"

"No of course not. What's cooking? I'm really hungry."

"I hope you don't mind but I've done a vegetable Mousakka. I had loads here so I threw them all in together. It'll probably taste awful. Pour yourself a drink. There's some wine on the table."

Ben watched her walk into the kitchen. She looked lovely, just how he'd imagined she would, as he'd sat on the bus coming into town. The Mousakka was delicious. Whatever Joanna had put in it made it taste really good. She talked about her job and the night before. What it was like having to speak in front of so many people.

Ben sat and listened thinking all the time how beautiful she looked, with her hair hanging straight down either side of her face. Her eyes flashed as she spoke and he felt he could see deep inside her mind. He felt comfortable with her as if this was where he was meant to be.

"Ben."

"Yes?"

"I wanted to talk to you last night, but I didn't get the change."

"You were drunk and then asleep. How could you?"

"I know. You see, it's my job. Last night, during the meal, I was offered a new job in London. It's in the Headquarters. Much better than what I've got now. Much better prospects too. Ben, I couldn't turn it down."

Ben was stunned. He'd seen this evening as something new, a beginning, not an end. He felt cheated and lost. Here was the one person he truly loved saying she's leaving."

"Say something, please Ben."

"I don't know what to say. I've got so used to you suddenly leaving I suppose I should have expected it. When are you going?"

"I've got to go up to London for two days tomorrow. Then I'll be back for two or three weeks to finish things off here. Sort the flat out as well and then I'm off. I'm sorry Ben. I couldn't seem to find the right time to tell you."

He didn't say anything. He got up and walked out to the balcony. It was raining. He stood gazing out to sea lost in his own thoughts. Was she really telling him this was the end or was there still a chance in the future? He couldn't get his head round what she'd said at all.

"Ben."

"What?"

"I am sorry. In my business you don't say no to an opportunity like this. If I don't go now, I'll never do it, I know I won't. I'll be back from time to time. Perhaps we could meet up then?"

"Joanna, I think I should go. You have everything sorted out. You're in the driving seat. Your future's secure. Thank you for the meal. I'll remember our times together for ever. Remember Joanna, I do love you. I'm sorry. I'll have to go."

With that he pushed past her and made for the door.

"Ben you can't leave like this. Please wait. Don't go yet."

Ben turned but knew he must go. He took one last look at those beautiful, stunning eyes and left.

Outside in the cold air his eyes filled up, he felt as if he was going to choke and his stomach twisted into a knot. He was shattered. He wanted to be as far away from Joanna as possible, but at the same time he wanted to be with her. Whatever she was doing, he still loved her, but at this moment in time he had to be on his own, with his own thoughts and feelings.

Ben just made the last bus. He wiped the tears from his eyes before getting on, sat in the first seat he came to and looked straight out of the window. Being the last bus it stopped everywhere but he kept his vision away from those people getting on and off.

The bus drew up at the bus stop next to the harbour. Ben got up after a couple of other people and got off the bus.

"Ben, what on earth's the matter with you? You haven't stopped staring out of the bus all the way home."

It was Jenny. She'd been on the bus all the way back and he hadn't noticed her. She had watched him get on and had noticed immediately how awful he looked. She knew him well enough to recognise that he was very unhappy and that something significant must have occurred. Presumably with Joanna.

"Oh Jenny, it's you. Were you on the bus? I'm sorry I didn't see you. Lost in my own thoughts."

"You certainly were. You look terrible. Are you all right?"

"I'm fine. Well, no Jenny, I'm not really. Had a bit of a shock."

"Joanna?"

"How did you know that?"

"Just a guess Ben. Can I help? You want to talk about it?"

"I don't know. No. You don't want to be bothered with my problems."

"Ben, haven't we known each other long enough to be honest with each other now?"

"Yes, I suppose so. Look, come and have a drink with me at my place. I've got to talk to someone about this. Anyway, why aren't you at work tonight?"

"I do have some time off you know. I went to see a film."

"Good?"

"No, not really. I'd rather have been at home writing my book!"

They walked the rest of the way to his house in silence. Once there Ben got them both a glass of wine and told Jenny about his evening. She sat, completely still at his feet, leaning on the arm of his chair taking in every word. She let him speak without interruption as she knew he had to explain his feelings before he'd be able to come to terms with what had happened.

"I'm sorry Jenny, I shouldn't be burdening you with all of this, but thank you for listening."

"Ben, it's just like those days when we were young, sitting on the harbour wall. Talking about our hopes for the future and what we would like to do. I keep telling you I'm always here for you, if you need to talk."

"Thank you Jenny, you always do seem to know what to say. You're very good at giving me the right advice."

"No Ben. You talk. I listen. You sort it out in your mind. You always have. That's why you're living here. You made the decision. Remember?"

"Yes. I know you're right, but sometimes I wish you'd tell me what to do."

"If I did that Ben, you'd probably get very annoyed and tell me to mind my own business. Now come on Ben. Look to the future. You've got the Sail Loft to sort out and don't forget Aunt Jessie."

"I know, I've neglected all that. I've been so caught up with Joanna. I've even stopped making my pots."

"Well, there you are then Ben. You know which direction to go in now. I must go. I've got to get up early, there's an order arriving."

"Thank you Jenny. I do appreciate the time you give me. Look, let me walk you home. I could do with the fresh air."

"All right, but I'm used to going everywhere on my own you know."

"I know. Come on let's go."

Ben walked Jenny the short way across the village to her house. She lived just above the beach car park and had a wonderful view out across the bay. They stood at the door step, Jenny looked for her key and Ben watched her as he always did. Jenny found her keys, looked up at Ben and gave him a kiss on the cheek.

"Goodnight Ben. Take care of yourself and remember, keep looking forward, not back."

"Goodnight Jenny. Thank you."

Ben kissed her on the cheek too. They squeezed each other's hands smiled and Jenny let herself in. She closed the door behind her. Ben turned away and walked home. He was very tired and fell asleep as soon as he was in bed.

Jenny, on the other hand, had remained with her back against the front door after she'd closed it. Her hand against her cheek where Ben had kissed it. It had made her shiver inside and she wanted to savour the moment. She'd always hoped that maybe one day she and Ben would be together, even from the days when they used to sit on the harbour wall. She'd never told anyone, but she knew that Jessie too had hoped they'd be together. Ben, however, as far as she knew, had never considered it. After all, there was only one person in his life at the moment, Joanna.

The next few days were difficult for both of them. Jenny, because she had felt something stir inside her when she was with Ben and Ben because Joanna was lodged permanently in his mind.

Jenny lost herself in her business and kept any feelings she may have for Ben out of her head until she was on her own at home. Ben on the other hand, found the feelings for Joanna all consuming. He found it increasingly hard to concentrate on anything. He was unable to sleep, but as soon as he awoke, Joanna's image was there and swept over him. Needless to say his work was suffering. He was way behind with his orders. When he began a pot he made unnecessary mistakes and had to throw it away.

As for the Sail Loft, to begin with it faired no better until Aunt Jessie decided she should take charge and organised Ben so much he daren't argue. At least once she had done that, he found he became so engrossed in what he was doing, that he could keep Joanna out of his mind for quite long spells.

The more Ben worked on the Sail Loft, the more he wanted to get it finished. Jessie was a great help and encouraged him all the time, not once saying he shouldn't sort things out as he wanted. He appreciated this freedom and was soon able to categorise everything and clear anything that was unwanted.

He shelved his pottery orders until after he'd finished the

The Sail Loft

Sail Loft and just hoped he didn't lose any of them. The Sail Loft became his main priority above all else and it had one positive advantage. He was able to put Joanna, if slowly at first, out of his thoughts completely. It was now only when he was alone that things washed over him and he felt helpless and the need to see her again. He also decided he was not going to be the first one to make a move. She'd made her decision and as Jenny had said to him, he must look to the future and move on. It was this he now felt he was doing by sinking all his efforts into the Sail Loft.

Ben also cut himself off from his friends. He hadn't seen George at all, didn't go in 'The Ship' for a drink or eat up at Jenny's. He spent most of his time with Jessie and her friends who kept calling round to wish her well in the future. The days flew by and that evening in Joanna's flat became a distant memory.

There came a point, however, when he knew he had to consult both George and Jenny over the Sail Loft's future. They had offered their support at the start and he knew he couldn't abandon them completely. He wanted, though, to have his own plan clear in his mind first and there was also the matter of the E-type Jaguar and the motorbikes, in the garages. George, he knew, had contacts in the antiques world, who would be able to help him auction the vehicles. That, he decided, must be the first step. As wonderful as the E-type was, there was no way he would be able to maintain it or pay the running costs. Cars and motorbikes had only ever been a passing interest for him and he would much rather a real enthusiast had them. They, after all, would derive much more pleasure from them than he ever would.

Jessie agreed. She knew that Tom had left them to Ben so that he could finance his pottery, but she could also see how much he wanted to make a success of the Sail Loft. Tom would have approved, and in some way that helped Jessie to give Ben the freedom to develop his own ideas on the use of the Sail

116

Loft. She could see in Ben the same enthusiasm and
determination that Tom had had when he, like Ben, set his
mind to do something. She kept that thought to herself and
encouraged Ben as much as she could in her own way.

Ben had been into George's shop to discuss the sale of the
vehicles. It had transpired that the best place to sell them was
in auction rooms in Bristol. The biggest problem then became
how to get them there. George and Ben went down to 'The
Ship' for a drink, but also to discuss what to do about the cars
and bikes with Jack. After all, he was the one who knew Tom
best and had helped keep the bikes in running order.

"Well, I am honoured. You two haven't been in here for
ages."

"No Jack, we know. We've both been far too busy with
other things."

"So I hear. How are you getting on with Tom and Jessie's
place?"

"Really well thanks Jack. It's partly to do with that, that
we are here now."

"Oh yes."

"We'd like your advice. In Tom's old garages we've got an
E-type Jag and two motorbikes. We've got to get them up to
Bristol to an auction. Any ideas?"

"Well firstly, I knew they were there, but Tom had sworn
me to secrecy. He was always afraid that someone would steal
them. However, Jessie lent me a key and I've been servicing
them regularly. They're all in running order as far as I know.
Mind you, I don't know about getting to Bristol."

"It's the only way we can get them there. Transport costs
are astronomical."

"How about someone with a trailer. They could take the
bikes. I'm pretty certain you could drive the E-type. Have you
tried it out yet? At least then you'll know if it's running well or
not."

"Look Ben," said George, "I'll go and see if I can find anyone with a trailer and you try out the car. Check with Jessie first about tax and insurance. We don't want you arrested do we?"

So that was what they did. George found someone surprisingly quickly, who had a trailer up at the Treganza's farm at the top of the hill out of the village. Harry Treganza knew George well, as well as Jessie and Tom, so he was only too willing to lend them his trailer. George had a tow bar on the back of his van and could tow it when necessary. The trailer was just the right size to take two bikes.

Ben meanwhile, had discovered that Jessie had kept all the paperwork on the E-type fully up to date. Also, which surprised him somewhat, he was a named driver on the insurance. All that remained to do now was to see if the car started and if so, how well it ran.

It was with some uneasiness that Ben unlocked the garage on what was to be 'test' day. He didn't want anyone with him, so that if he made mistakes driving, there was no-one there to criticise.

The car started like a dream and he edged it out of the garage onto the driveway. He let the engine run for a while before getting out and closing the garage doors.

Back in the car he gently revved up the engine, slipped the clutch and was away. Heads turned as he rather noisily moved through the winding village streets. Once out of the village he pushed rapidly through the gears and sped along the more open roads. The engine seemed to him to be running perfectly, but whether the car would reach Bristol was another matter.

The test run went really well and Ben was confident that it would reach the auction when required to do so.

"We heard you go through the village Ben," Jack said as he walked in the pub.

"I'm sure you did. I thought I'd better come and let you know how well it ran. It was absolutely wonderful."

"I suppose you'll want to keep it now you've driven it, won't you?"

"No Jack. I've no interest in cars and I couldn't afford the upkeep. I just need to know from you whether you think it'll drive up to Bristol. Will you take it out yourself tomorrow and see what you think?"

"I will Ben, but I think you'd better do the driving. You are the one that's insured."

So that was decided and the next day Ben and Jack took the E-type for another run. Jack checked it over before and after the run and gave it a clean bill of health. The auction in Bristol would be next.

Ben planned his journey carefully. Wherever possible he would stay on dual carriageways so that his speed would not hold up traffic too much, although he knew that there were several places, before he left Cornwall, where this wasn't possible. He also decided to go via the Tamar Bridge at Saltash so that he could stop in the car park on the Plymouth side. This would be to take a photograph of the E-type against the backdrop of Brunel's rail bridge. Thus having an example of exquisite nineteenth century design as a backdrop for that of the twentieth century.

George and Jack sorted the bikes out and Jessie decided she would come as a passenger with Ben. She had often done the same when Tom was alive and had also been his navigator on rallies. It was decided that Ben should set off first and George and Jack follow on later in case there were any problems with the E-type on the way. There weren't.

The scheduled stop at the Tamar bridges took place without a hitch and Ben photographed the car in front of the bridge. He took several, some with Jessie in too.

They had all planned to meet up at the Exeter service station on the M5 and this they did with Jessie and Ben only having to wait ten minutes for the others. They had lunch there before going on to Bristol.

Ben couldn't resist the opportunity of photographing the car again. This time it was in front of Brunel's Clifton Suspension Bridge. They took the vehicles to the auctioneers where they were to be stored overnight ready for the auction the following day.

Ben had a cousin in Bristol who lived at the top of St Michael's Hill, not far from the auction room. So they all stayed there overnight. Ben didn't see his cousin very often now as she spent much of her time abroad on business, but she was home at the moment and only too pleased to see them and be able to help.

The auction was due to start at eleven in the morning so they arrived early enough to be sure the car and two bikes were looking their best. They needn't have worried as there were many lots in worse condition than theirs.

The E-type and the bikes were near the middle of the auction. Ben found the sale rather tedious, whereas Jessie was making a note of what each item was selling for in the catalogue. George and Jack sat with Ben but were taking more interest in what was happening than he was.

Ben was surprised how many people were there bidding. Quite ordinary people. It was they, however, who seemed to have all the money. He decided that they were either dealers or were agents for millionaires!

Eventually their lots came up. For Ben this was the crucial moment. He listened and watched intently as bidding took place. It moved quickly and he was amazed how the auctioneer knew who was bidding and who wasn't. Suddenly it was over and Ben looked at the others and they looked at him. None of them except Jessie, could quite believe how much the car had sold for. She seemed to accept the price as what was expected.

How she knew, Ben never did find out. Maybe she had made discreet enquiries beforehand. If the sum raised by the Jaguar was a surprise to Ben, the two bikes raised between them even more. The right people appeared to be in the right place at the right time.

Ben couldn't take it all in. It was over. The car and the bikes were gone. All they had to do was pick up the cheque and be on their way home. They waited till the end of the sale before getting up from their seats. Ben rose first and turned to help Jessie. As he turned he caught sight of a face he knew sitting at the back of the hall.

"Jenny, what are you doing here?"

"I didn't want to miss out on all the excitement so I caught the early train up to Bristol. I only just made it. I expect you're really pleased with the outcome of the sale?"

"Yes I am. Surprised, but very pleased. Why didn't you come up with us yesterday?"

"I couldn't. I've a business to run remember and there wouldn't have been enough room anyway for me too. I'm going back on the six o'clock train."

"Really, so are Jessie and I. George and Jack are driving back now, but we're having a meal with my cousin first. Why don't you join us, she wont mind."

"Oh I couldn't do that Ben, she won't be expecting me."

"Don't be silly, you'll be very welcome. They're a very Bohemian family. People drop in all the time, don't they Jessie?"

"Oh yes Jenny, they'd love to meet you. They're very hospitable. Do come with us, it's only just round the corner."

So Jenny went with them, was welcomed as one of the family and had a thoroughly enjoyable afternoon.

By the time they caught the train, they were very tired. They spoke very little to each other and Jessie slept most of the way to Exeter. Jenny and Ben talked a little about how Tom used to take her for rides on the back of the bikes. How he had taught her to ride and how balancing on the bike she had found very similar to balancing on a surf board.

Ben was relieved when the train left Exeter as it had brought back thoughts of Joanna and the feelings he had for her. However, he was with Jenny and Jessie and got his mind back on them. He wandered up the train and managed to get a coffee for each of them, but nothing to eat. Mind you his cousin had fed them well so they weren't really hungry anyway.

Once Jessie was awake she talked non-stop about the day. She'd obviously thoroughly enjoyed herself. Ben meanwhile was thinking about the Sail Loft and how to turn it into a working environment. He'd switched off from Jessie's chatter. Fortunately she hadn't noticed as Jenny seemed to be saying all the right things.

The journey at least appeared to be passing quickly. Somewhere between Plymouth and Truro Ben took out his notebook and pencil and started to draw a plan of the Sail Loft. This immediately aroused the interest of the others. They in turn offered advice as to how Ben could make good use of each room.

It didn't help, although he tried to be patient with them and listen to their ideas. The last thing he wanted to do was offend them.

After the train left Truro they'd all had enough. The day had taken its toll. They spent the rest of the journey in almost complete silence. Ben had closed his notebook and was staring into the black abyss through the window, Jenny caught his eye now and again and smiled. Jessie slept soundly until they reached Penzance.

They took a taxi back to the village. Jenny and Ben walked Jessie home and made sure she was all right. They then walked to the sea wall and sat where they used to, gazing out to sea.

"Thank you for being there Jenny. I appreciate it. I hope it wasn't too boring."

"No, not at all. I enjoyed it. It was a real treat for me. I told you, I don't go out much."

"Do you know Jenny, the oddest thing about all this, is that I've got a cheque in my pocket for the car and bikes but I don't know who's bought them?"

"Perhaps that's the best way. At least you can't look at them and think, I don't want them to have my car."

"Yes you're right. I hadn't thought of it like that. It's been a long day, you must be shattered. Let me walk you home."

"Thanks Ben, I'd like that."

They walked round the edge of the harbour looking down at the water with it's reflections of the street lights bobbing about as the water ebbed and flowed. Outside Jenny's house they stopped. She looked up at Ben, smiled and gave him a kiss on the cheek. He returned the kiss and turned to go.

"Ben."

"Yes."

"Would you like a drink to celebrate?"

Ben looked at her as she said this and could almost see a pleading in her eyes.

"Yes, that would be a good end to the day."

Jenny's stomach turned over and her knees went weak. She couldn't believe he'd said yes and wasn't prepared for the reaction. She fumbled in her bag for the key, eventually found it and opened the door. Ben hadn't been inside before and was really surprised with what he saw.

"Where did you get all these from, you must have paid a fortune."

"They've all come from my family. We've always collected antiques. I love them. The settees are 1930's and I've collected the cushions over the years. It's my hideaway Ben. Where I can escape from work and the outside world."

He noticed too that there were no trophies from her surfing days or books that she'd written.

"I know what you're thinking Ben. Where are the books and trophies? Come through here."

Jenny opened a door that led into a smaller room which housed the missing items.

"There you are. This is my office or workroom. Whatever I want it to be. So you see, my past is still important to me, just as much as the present. Now let's have that drink."

They sat almost buried in the heaps of cushions talking about the times they'd had together and how each of them saw their future now.

"Ben, tell me exactly what you are going to do with the Sail Loft."

"Right, this is decision time is it?"

"It had better be. I'm fed up with waiting for you to make up your mind."

"Firstly, I'm going to have the ground floor of the Sail Loft as a café. Don't say a word Jenny. Secondly, upstairs will be everything I'm selling. Thirdly, I will let the cottage to holiday makers in the summer or all year round if I want. There you are Jenny, all complete at last."

"I don't think so Ben. It won't work and you won't be a success."

"Why not? You said you'd give me advice. Positive, not negative advice."

"I am Ben. You haven't thought it out properly. Here, pass me that notepad and pencil."

Jenny proceeded to draw a plan of Jessie's cottage and the Sail Loft. Ben sat watching her every move and was surprised at how well she knew every detail of the cottage.

"Now Ben, look at the plan and tell me the major problem."

Ben looked carefully at every area of the plan.

"You've got everything on it. I can't see a problem. It all seems to be in place to me Jenny."

"Right, I'll try it another way. You've converted the Sail

Loft, put in your café and let the cottage."

"Yes."

"I'm your first customer. Are you with me so far?"

"Yes Jenny, go on."

"This is where the problem comes in."

"Right."

"How do I get to the café and Sail Loft shop whilst there are people in the cottage on a holiday let?"

"Ah."

"Yes, ah indeed Ben. Where is the door or passageway access to the Sail Loft?"

"Now I see the problem. You are clever Jenny."

"No Ben, it's just common sense. The Sail Loft is upside down too."

"What?"

"The shop should be downstairs and the café up. Apart from that, I think you are on the right track Ben."

"Thank you Jenny. I haven't really planned it out very well at all have I? Can I take the plan you've drawn with me?"

"Of course you can. We must get together with George and really talk it through. Go and see him in the morning Ben and arrange it. Now off you go home. It's late and I'm tired. Thanks for coming in for the drink."

Jenny kissed him again as he opened the door. Again he returned the kiss and left. It was then that Jenny realised just how strongly she felt about Ben. She returned to the cushions and buried herself in them with tears streaming down her face. All these years she'd remained strong and determined not to let herself get close to anyone. Yet here she was falling in love with Ben. Ben who she'd grown up with. Ben who she'd always thought of as a brother. Ben who she knew was deeply in love with someone else. Joanna, who kept leaving him. Joanna he kept running to when called.

Couldn't he see how much she, Jenny, felt for him. No he

couldn't. His thoughts were elsewhere. The Sail Loft, his pottery and above all else, Joanna.

Ben on the other hand, had slept well and was up early loading pots into his kiln. The only thing on his mind was to get hold of George as early as possible and show him Jenny's plan for the Sail Loft. He knew he had to keep up with his orders from the exhibition, but he was finding it a struggle with everything else that was going on. Also, there was Aunt Jessie. She seemed to be staying much longer than he'd originally thought. If he had to make major changes to the Sail Loft, then he'd feel happier about it if she was in America with her daughter. Still, he couldn't force her to leave her own home and after all she seemed to be rather enjoying what was going on.

George was sitting behind the counter drinking tea when Ben arrived. There was no-one in the shop.

"Morning Ben. You're up very early today or haven't you been home yet?"

"I'm early George. I slept very well as it happens. Take a look at this will you?"

"What is it?"

"It's a plan of the Sail Loft. I made a fundamental mistake with my own. Jenny did this for me last night and before you ask, we had a drink to celebrate the sale."

"It looks very good. I like the lay out. What was wrong with yours Ben?"

"You couldn't get into it without going through the cottage. I'd forgotten about an entrance. By the way, I presume you had a good journey back from Bristol."

"Yes very easy. No problems at all. The trailer's gone back too. So now you can concentrate on developing this Sail Loft of yours."

"I know, but really it's the problem with the entrance that's bothering me most. I just can't seem to work out where to put it."

"I think Jenny's set you off in the right direction, but you've both forgotten something. Go over to the harbour entrance Ben and look back at your Aunt's cottage. The solution will be very obvious. If I can see it, then so will you."

Ben left the shop, walked along the road to the car park and out along the harbour wall. When he was opposite his Aunt's cottage he stopped. There was a bench nearby that he sat on. He took out the plan and looked across the harbour at the cottage. He looked carefully at the front door, the window, the roof and the cottage to the right of his Aunt's.

He couldn't see what George was on about. He let his eyes wander back across the front of the building towards the car park. Then it dawned on him. To the left of his Aunt's cottage was a wide passageway that led to a row of terraced cottages behind the Sail Loft. In front of them were small enclosed gardens. To reach these you had to walk through the passage under a huge granite plinth which held up part of the cottage next door. Once through this, you were in a garden so well kept that it was almost like an imaginary world.

Just as you reached the garden there was a gate that led into the courtyard of the Sail Loft. This would be ideal as an entrance and would enable Ben to fulfil his dream.

Back in the shop, George confirmed what Ben had thought. The next stage was to find someone to draw up decent plans and to make sure they had met the right planning regulations. This could still hold up Ben if he didn't receive the go ahead for the development.

The only person he knew who had any alterations done was Jenny. So he walked up to the café, found his favourite table that overlooked the harbour and picked up the menu.

"I thought you knew that off by heart Ben. Don't tell me, a cup of coffee and a toasted teacake, with raspberry jam."

"No Jenny, not today. I've been up for ages. Are you still doing cooked breakfast?"

"You never have that. Whatever's got into you today?"

"I did what you suggested and took the plans to George. We've sorted it all out now. I've come to talk to you about it. Have you got time to talk?"

"Do I look busy? Of course I can talk. Claire, get Ben a full English breakfast please. Right, now what have you decided?"

"When you bought the café you made quite a few alterations didn't you?"

"Yes."

"Well, who did the plans for you?"

"I did it initially. A bit like I did yours, but in much more detail. I took them to the planning department first to get their opinion and then to an architect who drew up the final plans. He also oversaw the work"

"Do you think he was good, this architect?"

"Of course, I'm really pleased with how everything turned out. I'll get his phone number for you."

Jenny left him to his breakfast and fortunately Claire didn't hang around chatting as some other customers had come in. Ben took out his plan and spread it on the table to one side of his plate. Everything seemed to be slotting into place. At last he felt his vision of how the Sail Loft should be was actually going to come to fruition.

Jenny came back with the phone number and Ben's coffee which Claire had forgotten.

"Ben, you make sure you phone him. He was a great help to me so tell him I recommend him to you. Right, let's have another look at these plans. I see you've managed to get your food all over them already. You don't change do you? I remember you doing just the same with some work you were doing as a holiday project when you were at school."

"Do you really remember that? Jessie made me write it all out again, it took hours."

"I remember because we'd all gone off to the beach and you were stuck inside."

"Enough reminiscing Jenny. What do you think?"

"It looks better now you've put in the proper entrance, but the tomato squashed in the front window doesn't help."

"No it doesn't. I'll have to draw it again. I don't suppose you'd give me a hand?"

"I wondered how long it would take you to ask! Look, I'll do you a deal. Tonight's my night off. You cook me a meal up at your place and I'll draw your plan for you. Is it a deal?"

"You drive a hard bargain Jenny. All right, it's a deal, but you'll have to put up with whatever I've got."

"That's OK. I'll eat anything provided it's cooked by an expert like you."

"Now you are joking Jenny."

"I'll see you later then Ben. I must go and give Claire a hand."

"See you. Come over after you've finished here, about seven."

"Yes, I'll see you then."

Ben folded up his plans, finished his breakfast, paid Claire and walked home feeling very pleased with himself. Almost to the extent whereby he felt as if everything was cut and dried and he needn't worry about anything anymore.

He left the plans on the kitchen table, went out to his workshop and spent the rest of the day making pots. He felt on top of the world, as if a huge weight had been lifted from his shoulders. The day went really well and Ben was surging through his order book and catching up on the backlog from the kiln. He'd taken out the pots he'd fired earlier and the new glazes looked very good. He was both surprised and relieved at the same time.

He became so engrossed in his work that he forgot all about the time. At four o'clock he made himself a drink and happened to glance at the clock. Suddenly it hit him. Jenny was coming at seven. What could he cook? He rushed around from his fridge to his freezer and back again. He'd jokingly said she'd have to make do with what he'd got. It wasn't a joke. He really didn't have enough to make a decent meal. He'd have to go into Penzance to the supermarket and he'd have to go by car to be quicker. He tried to avoid driving as much as possible, but at least parking was easy when he got there.

He grabbed his wallet and cheque book and left everything as it was. He didn't change and went as he was, covered in clay. The drive in was fine until he reached the town itself where he got stuck behind a tractor and trailer and the traffic lights held him up in the centre.

Whilst sitting there, waiting for them to change, he watched the people walking in and out of the shops. Just as the lights began to change he glanced at the estate agents where Joanna used to work. He wished he hadn't, for there, larger than life, was Joanna with her arm around someone who looked ominously like her husband. He recognised him from the newspaper.

His stomach turned over, he went hot and cold at the same time and his legs felt like jelly. He had to drive on. He daren't look back. He drove badly and erratically to the supermarket, got out of the car and forgot to lock it. He leant on the roof and took deep breaths of fresh sea air and tried to calm down. What was she doing there? Was this more lies? Had she never been away at all? Why were they together after all she'd said about their relationship? He couldn't come up with a reasonable answer for any of it.

He went to get a trolley and then remembered he hadn't locked the car. He went back, daydreaming, but trying to get what had happened in perspective.

He wandered round the supermarket quite aimlessly and when he got to the checkout wasn't sure what he'd actually bought. Neither did he have any idea what he was going to cook for Jenny.

He drove home in a complete daze. He put the shopping in the kitchen and walked out into the garden. He went right to the end, peered over the wall and looked down into the harbour.

It looked so peaceful and tranquil. He could see George going out in his boat fishing. Jenny's cafe looked busy and there were people sitting outside it eating ice-creams. He wished his own life was as easy, simple, straight forward and uncluttered. It wasn't. Joanna had seen to that. Now, here he was again wondering what she was doing and how truthful she was being with him. He longed for an easy answer, but there didn't seem to be one.

It was getting late and Jenny would be arriving soon. He still had no idea what to cook. Joanna was filling his mind. It was difficult to think of anything else. Here she was again, telling him one thing and doing another. He needed to confront her with it, but was frightened of the outcome. Although if he was really thinking straight he knew what his reaction ought to be. He should put her out of his mind completely. She was untruthful, deceitful, covert and in real terms, to him a complete bitch. So why couldn't he free himself of her? Why did she still have that affect on him? After all, she had never actually said she loved him. It was all one way. He was convenient. There at her whim and foolish enough to run when called. Maybe now he was beginning to see what she was truly like. Joanna was not for him. He would not contact her. If she phoned he would be cool and certainly would not go if asked to visit her. Powerful stuff all this, he thought to himself as he saw Jenny leaving her house and walk past the café and start up the road towards his cottage.

He dashed back inside and started to tidy up. He cleared a space on the table and spread the Sail Loft plans out carefully. Any rubbish he quickly threw into the bin in the kitchen. He fluffed up the cushions on the settee and chairs and picked up bits of clay that were dropping off his clothes. It was only then that he remembered what he was wearing.

The door bell rang. He ran and opened it.

"Hi. My goodness, you have made an effort Ben. I didn't realise it was a fancy dress do."

"Very funny Jenny. Come on in. I'm sorry, I haven't had time to change. I've been working all day."

"No time to unpack your shopping either Ben. I'll give you a hand."

"Thanks. I seem to have got all behind today."

"So I see. And what exactly are you cooking tonight? You've bought some very strange things. Do you usually cater for yourself like this?"

Jenny held up a large tub of nappy rash cream.

"Oh no! I must have seen cream and thought it would go with the fruit."

"Are you sure you know what you're doing Ben?"

"Well, I did when I left here to go shopping, but something happened on the way."

"You were attacked by aliens?"

"No of course not. I drove past the estate agents and looked in and…"

"You saw Joanna?"

"Yes, how did you know that?"

"She's the only person I know who gets you in a complete state of confusion. Did you stop and talk to her?"

"No, I drove on to the supermarket. She was with her husband."

"Oh was she now. Will you get in touch with her?"

"No."

"That was a very definite no. Are you sure?"

"Yes Jenny. I've been a real fool where she's concerned. I should have realised she wasn't really interested in me. I was just there when she got bored or on her own and of course I went to her as soon as she got in touch."

"Yes Ben, you did. I am sorry it's not worked out how you wanted, but I do think you've made the right decision."

"Do you really?"

"Of course I do Ben. Remember, as I keep telling you, I've known you a long time and I care about what happens to you. So does Jessie. We do think a lot about you even if we don't always say very much."

"Thanks Jenny. Come on, I'll cook us this meal, but I'd better get out of these clothes first. Get yourself a drink. I won't be long."

Jenny poured two glasses of wine and then set about trying to make some sense of what Ben had bought. She gave that idea up and sat at the table sipping her wine whilst looking at Ben's plans. She looked round the room too. She liked it here with Ben. It felt comfortable and homely.

"Right, I'm here and I'm clean. Thank you for unpacking everything. I really have bought some odd things haven't I! Ratatouille do you Jenny, or would you prefer something else?"

"You fool. Get on with it. I'll try and make sense of your drawings here."

They smiled at each other and both got on with their respective jobs. Ben prepared the vegetables, but kept sneaking a quick look at Jenny every now and again. She had left her hair loose and it fell in wavy lines over her shoulders. Every now and then she'd flick one side back as it got in the way. Ben watched entranced. He always was comfortable with her around, quite unaware that Jenny felt exactly the same.

Ben eventually prepared everything and left it to cook. Anything else they needed he would do later. He sat down at the table with Jenny. She looked up and smiled.

"Not bad Ben."

"The plan, the meal or me?"

"The plan you idiot. You've made a good job of it. I'm impressed. I've altered a few things, but I'll draw it out again for you so that it's clearer."

"Thanks Jenny. I'm still worried about taking trade from you and George though."

"I know you are, but don't worry. What you are doing is different. Once you get known, like I have, people will come here specially. It will help us all. You wait and see."

"I wish I had your confidence. Remember, this is all new to me. I'm bound to make a huge mess of it."

"Ben, I made loads of mistakes. So did George. After a while you begin to learn from them and turn them to your advantage. Don't worry. You'll be fine."

Ben left Jenny to get on with the drawing and went to check the food. When it was ready. Jenny put the plans carefully to one side so that there was room for them to eat.

"Ben, you have excelled yourself. This is wonderful. How do you get it to taste so good, even my chef can't do that."

"Praise indeed! I don't know. I made one two weeks ago and that was revolting and I threw it away. All I've done today is shop in a complete daze and whatever I remembered to get in the way of vegetables I've thrown in. So it's pot luck really and fortunately this time it's worked."

"Well, however you did it, it's really good. I'm impressed."

"Thanks. I like your hair like that."

Ben said this without thinking. It just seemed to be the most natural thing to say at that moment.

"Do you, why?"

This was the first time Ben had ever said anything like this to Jenny and it had taken her by surprise.

"I like the colour. I always have. You've grown it longer and it's falling around your face and over your shoulders and it sets off your features and…"

"That's enough Ben. Don't overdo it."

"I'm not. It's how you look. I was trying to find the right words."

"Were you now? Well thank you anyway. I usually keep my hair up because of work. I hadn't realised it was quite this long until tonight. I'll have to get it cut."

"No, don't do that Jenny. I really like it long. It suits you."

Jenny looked up at him across the table and smiled. Ben smiled back and caught a look in her eyes he'd never seen before.

"Right, these plans of yours Ben. You can do the washing up when we've finished and I'll redraw your plan. Is that all right?"

"Of course it is. I'm very grateful that you've found time to come and do them."

"If you serve up meals like this I shall be here more often."

Jenny looked at him again. The same look as before. Ben couldn't make it out. It certainly made him feel uneasy. He smiled, picked up their plates and went into the kitchen.

"I seem to have bought some fresh fruit. Would you like some?"

"What have you got?"

"Raspberries, strawberries and some raspberry ripple ice-cream."

"I'll have some raspberries and some raspberry ripple then please."

Ben filled two of his own pottery bowls and returned to the table.

"I like the bowls. Yours?"

"Yes, the old glazed design. I've come up with a new colour scheme for the latest batch. I still like these which is why I use them most of the time."

"Have you finished all your orders from the exhibition?"

"Nearly. I've a few more to glaze and then fire. After that I'll get back to my usual work."

"So you've done my order then?"

"Your order?"

"Yes. Surely you haven't lost it Ben. You do know my name after all."

Ben got up and ran out to the shed and returned with his list of orders.

"I can't see your name on here Jenny. There's no-one here called Jenny anything."

"Let me look."

Jenny took the paper from him and ran her finger down the list of names.

"There you are Ben. Right at the bottom of your list is my name."

Ben read it out loud as he put his finger on the name. 'Carnon G.J.' "Of course. I always forget the significance of your other name."

"You see Ben. I lead a double life. I am Jenny Carnon, owner of the café and restaurant. Elsewhere, I am Georgia Carnon, archaeologist and of course, the ultimate surfer with the slogan 'Surf with G.J.C. to victory.' There you have it Ben. You've always known me as Jenny and that's what I like the best. Now, where's my order then?"

"In the kiln, is the simplest answer."

"Prove it then Ben. Take me out to the kiln."

They went into the garden and into Ben's workroom.

"So this is where all the work is done then. Sometimes I wonder if you ever find time to do anything."

"Here's the proof Jenny. Each order numbered, labelled and priced. All I need to do is pack each one and send it off. Yours is still in the kiln cooling down. If I open the door too soon it'll crack the pots or damage the glaze."

"So when can I have mine then Ben?"

"Probably tomorrow evening. Look at the others here. Yours is very similar to them."

Jenny looked carefully at each pot and at the glaze.

"I'm impressed Ben. Seeing all these together makes me realise how much you've developed your style since you came here. I think at last you are finding what you moved here for. You're going to be a big success."

"Thanks Jenny. You haven't finished your meal. Come on in again. We've still got the plan to finish."

"Oh no, the ice-cream's melted. Still, I'll mush it up and it'll taste more like a fool!"

"Trust you, Jenny. Next thing we'll know is that you've introduced it on your menu."

"Hardly, I only eat things like this away from work. Now then Ben, you finish clearing up and make me a really hot cup of coffee and I'll get on with completing these plans."

So Ben pottered about in the kitchen whilst Jenny got on. Again, Ben kept looking at her and admiring her confidence and resolve to complete whatever she starts. He watched her hair swaying as she moved and as she flicked it out of her eyes. The auburn tints shimmered in the light and her eyes darted around as she drew on the paper.

Ben stopped what he was doing and leant back against the sink. He folded his arms and watched Jenny intently. There was something about her that he was seeing for the first time. The ease with which she coped with everything she did. The determination to succeed when presented with adversity. As he was thinking this Jenny looked up. Their eyes met and she smiled. He felt embarrassed that he'd been watching her, but smiled back and felt a gentle flutter in his stomach.

"You've stopped Ben." She said whilst carrying on drawing and looking down at the table. "That's not part of the deal."

"I've finished."

"Oh have you. Where's my coffee?"

"Sorry, I got carried away. I forgot."

"So I noticed. What were you watching so intently Ben? Me or the drawing?"

This really put him on the spot. He had been watching Jenny but he didn't want to admit it. However, it sounded from what she was saying, that she knew what he was thinking anyway."

"I'll be honest with you Jenny."

"I hope you will Ben. I don't like dishonest people, people who are not straight with me."

It was then that Ben knew he must tell her exactly how he was feeling. He felt suddenly that there was more to their relationship than just friendship.

"I was watching you Jenny. The way your hair was moving, its lovely auburn tints, the way you push it away from your face and how purposeful your eyes are. You seem so confident with yourself and able to cope with anything. I really admire that in you Jenny. You're a very attractive woman."

"Well that is telling me Ben. How long have you felt like this or has this just come into your head tonight?"

"It's built up over the last few days. Seeing you here tonight and having time to talk to you and look at you has helped me to see the real you I suppose."

Jenny got up from the table and walked over towards Ben. He watched her carefully. Her hair was long and flowing freely as she moved. She kept her eyes fixed on his until she was only a few inches away from him. They stood looking at each other. Ben could feel his heart racing and he wanted to touch her. She looked beautiful in a way he hadn't seen before. Was this the same Jenny he'd known for so long, or was it that she'd always been this attractive and he'd never noticed.

"Ben."

"Yes Jenny, what is it?"

"Ben, I need to say something to you, here right now, tonight. I can't keep it to myself any more."

"What is it Jenny? You look sad."

"Ben, I don't want to spoil our relationship, our friendship that we've had for so long."

"You can't do that. We'll always have that bond, our lasting friendship."

"I know Ben. Please listen to me."

Jenny put out her hands and held his. Ben's stomach fluttered again. She looked him straight in the eye again. Big, beautiful, piercing eyes that held him where he was.

"Ben I love you, and have for a very long time. I've tried so hard to hide it from you, but here tonight, I feel at home with you, relaxed and able to speak freely. Say something Ben, please."

She let go of his hands and stepped back. Ben looked at her and was able to see the love in her eyes. She did look beautiful in the subdued light. Thoughts of Joanna suddenly flashed through his mind, but he knew she was only using him. Was it Jenny who he should really be with? Why did he keep getting these feelings inside each time she looked at him? How foolish not to have seen this before. Here was someone who could really make him happy, who knew him so well and who loved him too. He knew he mustn't throw this chance away like he had others in the past. Now he realised just how much Jenny meant to him and how much he loved her too."

"Jenny."

"Yes Ben."

"I love you too."

Jenny flung her arms round Ben and gave him the most enormous kiss. Ben was washed away. He was in love. At last he knew what it really felt like.

They stayed locked together in each other's arms for fear of losing this precious moment. Neither of them wanting to let go in case it broke the spell.

Their friendship had lasted so long and yet only now did they realise the deep love they had for each other. A love that was so obvious that neither of them had seen it before. Their friends had seen it and wished it to happen. Jenny had realised it too but only since she'd seen more of Ben. Now he had to come to the same conclusion, that he and Jenny were made for each other and theirs was a deep and lasting love.

They still clung to each other but pulled back far enough to see each other's faces. Jenny had tears trickling down her cheeks, tears of joy and happiness.

"Jenny, why haven't we seen this before?"

"I think I have Ben, but you've been too preoccupied with someone else. You always have been. You asked me why I'd never married a while ago. Well, now perhaps you know. I've always felt close to you Ben and somehow it's stopped me getting involved with other people. I suppose in a way I've been waiting for you."

"How stupid I've been Jenny. If only I'd known, we could have been together long ago."

"No Ben, we couldn't. Too much baggage. The right time will always come along and now it has. You and I can now go forward together Ben, maybe even make some of those dreams come true too. I love you Ben."

"I love you Jenny."

They held each other very close and stood quite motionless for a few moments. Jenny spoke first.

"This won't get the Sail Loft developed will it?"

"No. It can wait. For once Jenny, I think we should be here for each other not for our businesses."

"Yes, you're right Ben. Maybe all that pushing you and goading you has worked."

"You used to be really awful and sarcastic."

"Yes, and now you know why. In fact, now I know why too."

"Because you loved me?"

"Exactly."

Jenny moved forward again and gave Ben a kiss on the cheek then turned towards the table.

"Where are you going Jenny?"

"Home. I've got a very busy day tomorrow even if you haven't."

"You can't go now Jenny."

"Why not?"

"Because it's not the right end to the evening. This evening, especially this evening. Just when we've found each other you can't walk away."

"Give me a good reason to stay Ben."

"Don't be silly Jenny. You're playing games again. Think what we've just been saying to each other."

"Yes I know. So what do you want to do Ben?"

"Jenny, I love you. Stay with me here tonight, please."

"I thought you'd never ask. Of course I'll stay Ben."

They were woken early by the gulls. Ben pulled back the curtains and the sunlight fell across Jenny's face. She looked as beautiful as ever. How could he have been such a fool as not to have noticed before. He gazed out across the roof tops. There was a mist hanging over the harbour. He turned and looked at Jenny again. She was watching him. They smiled and he slipped back into bed.

"I thought for one awful moment you were going to get up."

"No Jenny, not today. I've all I need here next to me. I love you Jenny."

"I love you too Ben, very much, but I will have to get up soon. I've a business to run remember?"

They lay together listening to the gulls each lost in their own thoughts. Ben squeezed Jenny's hand and she rolled over and put her head on his chest.

"Do you know Ben, I've dreamt of being here with you so many times. I can't believe this is actually happening."

"It is Jenny and you are here with me and I'm very glad you are. I just wish I'd realised before now that I felt like this about you. You're not suddenly going to disappear are you?"

"No Ben, I leave that to other people. I think you've had more than your fair share of vanishing women recently!"

"Yes, I take your point. Jenny, you will still work with me on the Sail Loft won't you?"

"Of course, why ever not? Even more so now. I think we need to tell Jessie about us don't you?"

"Yes, I suppose we will. She'll be absolutely delighted that all her scheming has paid off!"

"Now that's not fair Ben, she only wanted to see you happy. She hoped it would be the two of us because we've known each other so long. You never know, she might actually leave for America now if she thinks you're finally settled."

"It would certainly make the alterations at her cottage a lot easier if she did. Having said that though, I will miss her."

"We all will Ben, me more than you in a way. After all I have known her all my life. She's always been around."

"I know she has, but maybe this is the time for us all to put the past behind us and look to the future. After all, that's what Jessie is doing. So maybe we should do the same."

"Yes Ben, you are right, and another thing…"

"What?"

"It's time we got up. Come on, I've got to open up the café and you've those orders to send off."

They got up, had breakfast and went their own ways. Jenny to open the café and Ben to load orders into his car. Ben watched Jenny as she hurried down the road. He now knew he was with the one person who could make him truly happy. She turned at the corner, waved, blew him a kiss and was gone.

The phone rang. Ben picked it up. It was Joanna. He couldn't believe it. What timing. He listened as she went on about her job in London, how time consuming it was, who she'd met and how she'd not been able to get back to Penzance to see him. This, of course, he knew wasn't true.

"Anyway Ben, I thought it would be great if we could meet up again. How about dinner tonight?"

"I'm sorry Joanna but I'm busy tonight. I've got to come into Penzance this morning. I'll have a coffee with you if you're free."

"Oh, well all right then. I'm rather busy but could meet you. Where?"

"In the Arts' Centre. I've a delivery of pottery to make there at eleven o'clock."

"Right, I'll see you there. Bye."

Ben surprised himself with how assertive and positive he'd been. It was all Jenny's doing, but at least he was now more confident about dealing with Joanna's deceit. He packed the car and drove slowly through the village taking a quick glance up at Jenny's café, but didn't see her.

Ben had delivered one or two orders before he reached the Arts' Centre. He carried his pottery in and left it with Chloe who ran the sales side of the centre, before finding an empty table in the café at the back. He took out his notebook and ticked off the deliveries he'd already made.

"Hello Ben."

He looked up. Joanna stood in a black suit that hugged her figure. Her hair was tied back and her eyes as always flashed and sparked.

"You look well. Can I get you a coffee?"

"Thank you. Oh Ben."

"Yes."

"I'd love some flapjacks. It always was good here."

Ben brought two coffees and two pieces of flapjack back with him and sat down opposite Joanna. He looked up and their eyes met. He was lost, just as he always had been in her company."

"How have you been Ben? Work going well?"

"I'm fine thanks. I've just finished the orders from the

exhibition in Exeter. It was very lucrative."

"Good, I'm pleased. How's your Aunt? Has she gone to America yet?"

"No, not yet but very soon now. I've finished the plans for the Sail Loft and we're submitting them to make sure we can do the alterations we want."

"Who's we Ben? Have you got an architect in to help?"

"No, Jenny who runs the café and restaurant in the village is helping me. She's done all this before so her advice has been invaluable."

"Oh I see. Your friend George helping too is he?"

"Yes, on the business side. Everyone's been really helpful. I really must get on with my deliveries. It's been really nice seeing you again."

"Is that it then? I'm here for a few days Ben. We could have that meal."

Ben couldn't resist it any longer.

"How about your husband? Won't he have something to say about it?

"My husband Ben? I told you before that there's..."

"No Joanna. No more lies. No more excuses. I saw you together in Penzance. I'm not falling for that one again."

With this, Joanna slumped back in her chair and burst into tears.

"I'm sorry Ben... What can I say? You know how it is. You meet someone and things go from there. That's what happened when I met you. I've always lived quite an independent life. My husband's the same."

"Until you moved to London Joanna. Now you're back together again aren't you?"

"Yes. How did you know?"

"Things that were said at the dinner in Truro and the fact that you've put your flat on the market. You see, I do read the papers. Local girl appointed to big position in London with a picture of you both together. Rather a giveaway don't you think? No Joanna, I fell for you once. Not again. Goodbye."

With that Ben walked away from the table and out of the Arts' Centre into the fresh breezy air. He got into the car and drove straight off not daring to turn round in case he saw Joanna. He still couldn't quite believe what he'd done, but he did feel at least that he'd dumped the past and could look forward to the future with far more confidence. Joanna had deceived him more than once, he was going to make sure it didn't happen again. With Jenny, he would be open and honest and he knew that she would be with him. She always had been, he knew that already. After all the time they'd known each other, how else could they be?

Joanna on the other hand stood nonplussed at the table, still with coffee cup in hand and her mouth wide open. A few other customers noticed her, but paid little attention. She sat down and finished her coffee. No-one, not anyone, had ever dared do this to her before. She had always left the men, not the other way round. This was a new experience for Joanna and she didn't like it. The waitress came over with the bill. Ben had left without paying. This infuriated Joanna even more. She paid the bill and left.

Outside she looked around. There was no sign of Ben or his car. At last it began to dawn on her what he had said. How definite he had been and how angry he was with the way she'd treated him. She walked away from the Arts' Centre mumbling something about plenty more fish in the sea and he's welcome to his little café owner, but not audible enough for anyone to hear.

Ben meanwhile had completed his deliveries and returned to the village. He'd parked his car and briefly gone inside his cottage to leave the receipts from his orders. He left again almost immediately and walked to the café. Despite his new relationship with Jenny, Ben, from force of habit, sat at his favourite table in the window and looked out across the harbour.

He felt different. Almost light hearted and wanting to laugh out loud. He smiled as he watched the fishing boats come into the harbour.

"Can I join you Ben? You look pleased with yourself."

"Thank goodness it's you Jenny. I've just seen Joanna in town."

"Oh have you."

"Don't worry. I told her how I felt and that I didn't want to see her again. For me, I was very definite and I don't think she liked it."

"Well, I am seeing a new side of you. Two big decisions in as many days, whatever next?"

"Hopefully developing the Sail Loft and getting it opened."

"You've almost done that Ben. Go ahead and do it. I know it'll be a success. Stay here, I'm going to get us both a drink. When I come back we'll get you organised. No more putting things off. The Sail Loft is your main priority, then you can get back to your pottery. All right?"

"Yes Jenny. You are wonderful."

"No I'm not. I'm just practical."

Ben watched Jenny walk away and into the kitchen. She really did look wonderful. Yet again he couldn't see how he hadn't noticed all this before. How foolish he had been to keep pursuing Joanna when he hardly ever saw her. Somehow he'd kept a relationship going that just wasn't there.

Ben looked out of the window again and realised how lucky he was to be living in such an idyllic place, to have the friends he had and the opportunity to develop the Sail Loft. If only he'd seen what was now staring him in the face, then maybe everything could have worked out much quicker.

Lost in his own thoughts Ben stared out across the harbour watching the gently rippling water as the tide came in. Some of the boats moored there were still above the water line, but the rest were already pulling at their mooring ropes. The sun came and went as dark clouds raced across the sky, sending shadows from one side of the harbour to the other.

He watched the fish being unloaded. Only small catches these days, but none the less valuable. Gulls dived towards the catch hoping to pick up scraps and Ben let his mind wander. Back to the time as a child when he spent holidays here with his Aunt and Uncle and first met Jenny. A time when nothing mattered but the day you were enjoying. When he and Jenny sat talking on the sea wall, planning what they would be and guessing at the future. A future neither of them could have predicted would have turned out like this.

"Here you are Ben, a large mug of coffee without something to eat. Now, let's get organised. You look as if you've seen a ghost."

"No, I was miles away thinking about the past. You know, when we were young and all the plans we used to make. Funny how it's all turned out."

"It's not funny Ben, its lovely. I think we've always known somewhere deep inside that we would be together one day.

"Do you really? How can you be so sure?"

"I'm not, but somehow our relationship now feels right to me Ben. As if it was meant to be."

"I understand that, but it all seems to have happened so suddenly, I'm not sure it's sunk in yet."

"It will Ben. Maybe you need to rid yourself of someone else first, but I'm not going anywhere. I'm here for you Ben. I do love you so much."

"I know you do Jenny. I have cleared Joanna from my mind now. After this morning I know I could never go back to her. Jenny, I'm all yours. I love you too."

With that, they held hands and drew close to each other. They smiled and kissed, a long lingering kiss, each knowing what the other was feeling. As their lips parted, Ben pushed a parcel across the table towards Jenny.

"Something I promised you a while ago."

Jenny smiled at Ben and eagerly removed the paper.

"Oh, Ben! It is perfect. What else could it have been but you and me sitting on the seawall."

"Yes, it had to be really didn't it, I thought you could put it here on the window sill, overlooking the harbour."

"Of course, looking out at the spot where we used to sit, dreaming our dreams. Thank you Ben, it's been worth the wait!"

The next few days were hectic. Ben hardly saw Jenny as he whizzed around trying to finally sort out the Sail Loft. Aunt Jessie decided that she would leave for America as soon as possible, now that Ben seemed to be settled. The final plans were signed and work could begin on converting the Sail Loft.

Jenny meanwhile, insisted that Ben should use the same builder who had altered her café. He had done such a good job and was very reliable. Ben didn't argue. It was something else he didn't have to think about. Also, Jenny had known Dave Brison all her life, as he too had grown up in the village and she would much rather give the job to someone local.

So Jenny contacted Dave and he looked over the plans. He made one or two suggestions, but generally could see no problem with what Ben wanted.

Jessie was making the final preparations for her departure. She had insisted that Ben should not travel up to London to see her off. She was determined to make all the arrangements herself and travel alone from Penzance on the train. Despite everyone offering to go with her she insisted that she was quite happy to travel alone. It was good practice for the plane.

It was an emotional send off for everyone concerned. Jessie was so well loved in the village and here she was leaving to start a new life with her daughter in America. The night before she left, Jenny had open house at the restaurant and Ben lost count of how many people came. Neither Ben nor Jenny had a chance to talk to Jessie during the evening, but she had insisted that only they accompany her to the station. That is what Ben and Jenny did.

"Now listen you two. I don't want any sad farewells. For all three of us it's a new beginning. I shall be fine as long as you two keep me closely informed about what's happening in the village."

"Of course we will Jessie, and I'll make sure Ben lets you know all about the Sail Loft."

"You didn't have to say that! Of course I will Jessie."

"Now don't you two start arguing or I won't go."

"All right, we won't. Anyway Jenny doesn't have to boss me about and wind me up anymore!"

"As if I would. If anyone's doing the winding up it's you!"

"Now look here you two, my trains coming in. Let me know how you both are, won't you? I'm so pleased you're together at last and remember, if you decide to get married, I'm coming to the wedding! Now come on, help me with these bags."

Ben and Jenny did as they were told before they had a chance to comment on Jessie's statement. They just looked at each other and smiled.

All too quickly Jessie was gone and they were left holding hands on the empty platform. They looked at each other again and wrapped their arms round their shoulders.

"If it wasn't for Jessie we wouldn't be together now Jenny."

"Oh I think we would Ben. After all you made the first move remember. That took a lot to do particularly as you still liked someone else at the time and Jessie wasn't there then was she?"

"You're right Jenny. I do love you, you know."

"I know Ben, and I love you. Come on, back home, we've work to do."

The Sail Loft

They both turned and looked down the empty platform. Jessie was gone. They linked hands and walked out of the station into the bright sunlight of the day.